Abandoned

The story of boys forgotten

G. C. DE PIETRO

Artist and art therapist G. C. De Pietro follows the lives of four boys through their time in a residential treatment center. She thought she could help them but soon came to realize they taught her more about life, love and the pursuit of family values than she had ever dreamed possible.

Order this book online at www.trafford.com
or email orders@trafford.com

Most Trafford titles are also available at major online book retailers.

Printed in the United States of America.

ISBN: 978-1-4669-8459-2 (sc)
ISBN: 978-1-4669-8460-8 (e)

Trafford rev. 03/17/2014

 www.trafford.com

North America & international
toll-free: 1 888 232 4444 (USA & Canada)
fax: 812 355 4082

This book is dedicated to all the lost boys, who find the will and the stamina from deep within their souls to survive.

All of the names, dates, places and points of reference have been changed to protect the innocent.

Contents

List of Illustrations

Throwaway Society, Thrown-Away Boys

*W*HEN DID IT BECOME so widespread and tolerated to not be responsible for yourself or for your children? Is it just in these days of drug-induced amnesia, or has it been since the beginning of time that this indifference to your own flesh and blood has been so prevalent in society? How do you turn your back on your own children? Or, worse yet, abuse and neglect them and deprive them of the right to be nurtured and cared for?

I didn't think that the level of deprivation that I witnessed was possible until I came face to face with the children who lived in the residential treatment center where I worked and where I tried to restore their dignity. These are the thrown-away boys, the unwanted boys who so desperately wanted to be loved, who I came to know and respect.

It all began when I started working on my master's degree for art therapy. At that time, I volunteered during the summer months that I had off to work with boys at this residential facility because I wanted to hone in on the skills I had been taught. To be honest, I was intimidated by the entire situation, afraid that I might have to face my worst fears, the dreaded gang member or the street thug who, under different circumstances, might mug me or stab me in the back. Would I be safe working with them, or would my life be in danger? Of course, only time would tell, but I was nevertheless open to finding out if what I had been taught, that the art process could actually reach down into the depths of one's soul and heal them was real.

My first assignment was a group of adolescent boys in one small house who were all arsons; they had been neglected, alone and outcast from society. Initially, they viewed me with suspicion, and why wouldn't they? None of the people in their lives up to this point had done right by them so why would I be any different?

They didn't seem to trust easily and, worse yet, hadn't had a lot of creative outlets. Since most of these kids hadn't spent much time in school, either due to living in the street or simply being truant, they hadn't been exposed to the arts all that much and they were all behind in their studies. So, naturally, art was not the first thing on their mind.

These kids needed to learn how to read and how to be sociable, never mind how to be artistic. So here I was like an alien from another planet trying to do art with kids when they had no interest in doing so. None of these kids could go to their district school because their behavior was so abhorrent; they were being tutored in-house.

I was a volunteer working alongside the teachers and resident staff in the same house where the boys lived. I wasn't allowed to look at any of the boy's records. I was given a name, and that was that.

The atmosphere was rather tense, twelve boys in one small house. The dormitory-style rooms where upstairs. I never had any reason to go up there so most of my time was spent on the first floor.

When you first walked into the residence, there was a foyer with a desk, and one person would be scheduled to sit the desk at all times. Here they would take calls, make sure the boys were kept on schedule, and take inventory on things like if the boys got up on time for breakfast, took their showers, did their chores and so on. There was a point system in place within the residence where the boys could redeem their points for rewards at the end of the week, so the points really mattered to them. Staff would also make a note if any of the boys caused an outburst or refused to take their medications or anything that wasn't according to routine that would be a minus point.

Very rarely did anything ever go according to plan. Boys would fight; they seemed to look for confrontation at every turn. What became apparent as time went on was that none of the boys wanted to be there, so they would look to undermine whatever it was the staff wanted them to do. Even if they had no other home to go to in their minds they would often create fictitious scenarios like, that of the loving mother who was waiting at home for them to come back, or a foster home that was like something out of a fairytale.

The first day I arrived I was introduced to the boys as an art therapist who wanted to do summer projects with them. I met them in the dining room which had four tables in it, with room for staff to accommodate them while they had their dinner. The kitchen was open to the dining room so staff could keep their eyes on the boys while they ate.

There were about four to five staff members on at all times; depending on how many kids were in the house, it was about a ratio of three kids to one staff member. Two of the staff members were the director and assistant director, they had their offices in the basement, where they spent most of their time filing paperwork, doing most of the organizing of court dates, making doctor's appointments, arranging family visits, scheduling extracurricular activities, and filling out official documents. They were both social workers, and, whenever there was a disturbance such as a restraint, there was an investigation and a mountain of paperwork to process.

They were busy most of the time, so there were three/four other people up stairs who kept everything moving according to the plan of the day; they were what I call line staff. They were disciplinarians to the boys who kept them in line, made sure they were safe and had them follow schedules, do their chores and follow the rules.

They were also on hand to mentor the boys get them up on time for school, make sure they took care of their personal hygiene and tried to keep peace in the house. They were on around-the—clock, twenty-four hours a day, mostly, eight—hour shifts because you could never leave the boys unattended. I thought they had the hardest job of all and many of the line staff were like surrogate parents to the boys, and, overtime you could see alliances being made. If a staff member gave one boy more attention than another, jealousies would arise; fights would break out just like real siblings would, but these kids were all starving for attention, so the stakes were much higher and the antics for being top dog, pretty high as well.

There was also a living room where the boys could relax, watch TV and play board games or whatever. That is where I would meet the boys during the day for one on one time while most of the other kids were outside. There was also one other room, a class room, which had one teacher and an aid five days a week.

Even though it was summer, these kids went to school year round because they were all so behind their grade level they needed to catch up. It was not unusual to see a boy come flying out of the room with the teacher screaming at him to go for a time out. Even though there were twelve boys, living in this particular house only six of them would be in that classroom on any given day. The others would have class in the main school on the campus.

One boy named Alessandro, who had an innate interest in drawing, was one of the first boys assigned to me. He seemed to be very pleasant natured, with a slight build and a good sense of humor. He was very handsome with dark piercing eyes and tall for his age about 5'7" thin, with long, slender fingers. He was quiet most of the time and liked to stay by himself. He hadn't been there that long, and I didn't think he had bonded with anyone in particular.

Since it was summer, I was the alternative activity for the boys, allowing them to experience some pastime other than the usual basketball or baseball. Alessandro came to me because he wanted to learn how to draw, so at least he was receptive to my inquiries and tolerant of my presence.

I learned that his ethnic background was an interesting blend of Hispanic and European. I also learned a lot about him overtime because he was willing to go the distance with me because he seemed to want to turn his life around. Alessandro was talented, smart, funny and very streetwise. He could pick your pocket faster than you could blink an eye; at times I felt I was with the Artful Dodger from Charles Dickens's *Oliver Twist*. Come to think of it; the whole gang of kids could have been part of Fagin's motley crew, but, at least this time around, they were well fed and clean.

I felt that this was a young boy who was sensitive, perhaps too sensitive for what life had handed him. I liked Alessandro but had to be careful not to show him too much attention because the other boys would react negatively toward him, and I didn't want to cause him any trouble.

I wasn't sure how he would react to me at first. Remember, he was in a residential treatment center away from his family and friends, and I was the intruder. Who was I to come into his life and start asking questions?

I felt that this was the kind of situation that needed tact, timing, and, most of all, patience. I had to let Alessandro start to feel comfortable with me; there was no need to push him in any direction. We needed to get to know each other.

Before I knew his background, I wondered where I would start with him, how I would get to know him. We had one thing in common; he liked to draw and so did I.

So I started by playing a game with him. I would draw a scribble and he would have to turn it into something. Then he would draw a scribble, and I would have to turn it into something.

It was fun, and I found out that Alessandro was very imaginative and spontaneous, with a quick wit. He was beginning to unwind around me and let his guard down a little.

In fact, he wanted to learn how to draw because it helped him relax. He was very nervous and suffered from PTSD (Post Traumatic Stress Disorder) I remember thinking, "He is only fourteen years old; how in the world did this happen? What terrible things did he experience? Why would he trust me enough with his secrets, and if he did trust me, how would I be able to help him?"

Alessandro was such a sweet boy, tall with dark curly hair and those eyes that seemed to say,"Please don't let me down like all the others have." He was nervous; his hands would often shake, and he was always looking behind him, as if he were waiting for something terrible to happen.

When I asked him about his hands shaking, he said he couldn't remember a lot of things and didn't know when it had started but felt that he had this nervousness because of the medication the agency had put him on. I didn't have any of that information but knew that he was quite agitated when he came into custody. He told me he was in a juvenile detention facility when he first got picked up, but he didn't' tell me why.

We both agreed that this was not the worst place in the world he could have wound up and he certainly liked it better the Juvenile Detention Center. Nevertheless, he still missed his friends and family.

I tried to focus Alessandro on some of the good things about his placement. He was in a natural setting away from the noise of the city; he had three square meals a day; he didn't have to leave the campus to go anywhere, and there were plenty of outdoor activities. All the sports you could want were available, and, I must say, the staff went out of their way to make it as homey as they could for the boys.

Still, he missed his family, which made me wonder, "If his family was so terrific, how did he wind up in a place like this?"

We went outside, since it was summer, and did some sketching. He had natural talent; there was no doubt about it. If only he could control his hands from shaking, he would be able to draw a lot better.

Usually, when a boy first arrives, he is evaluated by one of the psychiatrists. He is then prescribed whatever medication they feel is appropriate. The plan is usually to have the boy put into therapy while the medication tries to stabilize his mood and affect. Overtime, after the therapy begins to help him develop coping skills and insight into his condition, the medication would be reevaluated, and in time the goal would be to diminish the amount of medication or eliminate it all together.

Since he had only been there for a few months, his medication was newly prescribed, and he wasn't used to it yet; hopefully, it would eventually be reevaluated to a more tolerable level.

Some of the boys would make fun of Alessandro because he liked to draw, but when they saw that he could command a lot of attention from the staff for the beautiful drawings he was creating, they thought, "Wow, how can I learn how to do that?"

Since I was a volunteer I didn't have an office. I was only there about ten hours a week, long enough to get to know the boys and do some art projects with them. I brought materials with me that was easy to cart around. I worked mostly out of my car. Paper, pencils, watercolors and markers weren't that expensive, and I had enough supplies to service the twelve boys in this particular residence. So it wasn't that much of a sacrifice for me to bring the art materials with me, and the house had some supplies that I could use as well.

I worked with Alessandro one day a week for an hour, saw one small group of boys, which Alessandro was also a part of for one hour a week, and worked with a couple of other boys who wanted to see me on a one-on-one basis as well.

The boys liked to be outside, so, on the days that were warm and sunny we would go out and sketch. Then, on the rainy days, or days when you needed to get some shade, we would use the living room in the house. Of course, when Alessandro and I worked together, we wanted to have some privacy, without people running in and out asking us a lot of questions. And, of course, we didn't want to listen to the staff disciplining other residents who were having difficulty. It was hard enough to have a kid with (ADD) Attention Deficit Disorder focus without all these other distractions, but we managed as best we could just the same.

On one occasion, I asked Alessandro what he missed the most. He said he had one friend back at home who he did everything with, who he trusted. He really missed that friendship because he did not really trust any of the other residents. They all had sordid backgrounds and problems of their own.

I asked Alessandro to draw me a picture of him and his friend together doing something. He drew a picture of the two of them playing at the top of a cliff that overlooked the ocean. He wanted to go swimming and dared his friend to jump into the ocean with him. They both jumped in and started swimming together.

This story seemed to be prompted by the hot summer sun. Alessandro said he and his friend had many places they would go swimming either by the river, or at the park near his house that had a lake, a stream, and also a pool.

This drawing started a series of drawings that conveyed a storyline and would continue every time we had a session. Evidently, the two boys liked to do dangerous things together. This cliff he drew was so high, and the ocean, so difficult to swim in; you either had to be very brave or a little crazy to jump. The cliff was way higher than the high dive at the pool, but his imagination brought him to this place.

This dramatic and dangerous jump seemed to be a reaction to being restricted in this residential setting, isolated from everything he knew; he seemed to just want to bust out and leap. The story as you will see takes him to the island in the Caribbean, where his father's family was originally from. So he swam across the ocean, urging his friend to keep up with him. But his friend couldn't do it. He turned back, saying the waves were too big and the journey, too long for him to go the distance. And so he left Alessandro alone to continue the journey on his own.

This was exactly what had happened to him. Alessandro had to travel unchartered territory without his friend. He had to go it alone, and it was dangerous, and he was afraid, but what else could he do?

Once he was in the middle of the ocean, he had to continue or turn back as his friend did, or drown. There are no other choices. If he turned back, he would be right back in the same desperate situation he was in at the beginning when he felt compelled to jump, so that was not a solution. If he stopped swimming, he would die, and that would be the end of the story but the story continued. He had a lot to say, he had his whole life ahead of him, he wanted to live.

The good news was that he had the energy to move on. If a ship had come by to save him, that would have been a happy ending, but it seemed as if Alessandro had to save himself. This was his journey, and he had to go the distance.

Alessandro had a plan, a destination, and, each week, when he came into session, I would ask, "And then what happened? And then what happened?" and so on. And, each week, he would draw an elaborate drawing that would take him farther and farther along his journey.

Eventually, he made it to the shoreline of this island. He fell onto the sand exhausted, not being able to move from having swam so far. He wasn't sure where he was, but after a while, he started walking and he came to a point in the beach where there was a marking that indicated he needed to climb upward.

There was another steep cliff, like the one he jumped from but now he had to climb to the top of it. This was very difficult, and it took a long time, but when he was about half way up to the top, a man called out to him and said, "Do you need a helping hand?" Alessandro replied, "Yes," and the man threw him down a rope and said, "Tie this around your waist and I'll pull you up."

Eventually, Alessandro made it to the top and found himself in a place he remembered, a place he had been to before in his childhood. It was a house that had a beautiful garden with fruit trees and very lush flowers, a place he remembered going to in the Caribbean, a house that was owned by his grandfather.

The older man asked him, "Why didn't you take the road?" and he responded, "There's a road?" Then the grandfather said, "You look tired; you need a rest." The boy replied, "Yeah, a long one." The grandfather said, "I have a room set aside for you I'll show it to you."

This was the first time he had mentioned his grandfather, but, now, I could see that this was a man he looked up to; the man he dreamt would be able to save him. In his drawing, his grandfather was the one who threw him the rope because he knew how exhausted he was. He knew, without his help he might not make it.

When he asks him why he didn't take the road, we realize that there was another way, an easier way to get to the grandfather. But Alessandro had to do it the hard way. The important thing was that Alessandro knew he could depend on him and that he would be there for him at the end of his long journey.

This was a major breakthrough for me because, now, Alessandro was starting to open up and talk about his family, his needs, and his desires. He didn't want to be alone. He wanted to be able to trust someone, and he was putting all of his faith into this one man, his grandfather.

He had a place for him in his house; in the drawing, the house was huge, indicating how important it was. This boy who seemed to feel like an outcast wanted to be part of a home and a family.

I wondered where Alessandro's parents were and why he couldn't depend on them. Will his grandfather really be there for him, or was Alessandro setting himself up for a huge disappointment? I could only hope and pray that he wouldn't be let down again.

I wanted his grandfather to be there for him. I wanted Alessandro to be able to cross the divide, bridge the gap, swim across the ocean to get to the one person who could help him, whom he trusted. What a daunting challenge to have to undertake. Alessandro felt like he had to cross an ocean to get what he needed.

What I needed to know was whether or not it was a total fantasy, thinking that his grandfather would be able to save him; or had Alessandro imagined this because he had nothing else to hold on to?

The summer was almost over, and I had to report back to my house supervisor. They hadn't asked me about what I was doing with the boys, but they could see that they were engaged, doing some beautiful artwork and staying out of trouble. Everyone, as far as I could tell, was content with whatever I was doing.

Finally, I was able to get the director and the assistant director of the house together in one room at the same time so that I could discuss with them my work with the boys. I had prepared my presentation and I had the artwork to back up my findings, using Alessandro as my test case.

. C. De Pietro

I explained that he was a boy who felt deserted by his friends and family, that he was sensitive and talented but misguided. He felt alone and needed to reconnect with his grandfather, who he felt was the only person who was really there for him. I felt that Alessandro was out on a limb, and if he didn't connect with him, I was afraid that he could have a psychological break. He had had a troubled childhood, and even though I didn't know the specifics of it, I knew it was traumatic enough to give him PTSD symptoms, such as nightmares and flashbacks. I backed up my findings with the drawings that he had done.

As I was speaking the director sat there shaking his head while his assistant stood there with her mouth open. Finally, she looked me in the eye and said, "How do you know so much about this boy in just a few weeks without having looked at his chart and not having spoken to anyone about him?"

I said, "Well it's all here in the artwork." I showed her the drawings and told her the meaning behind the symbols, and they were both stunned. Then they asked me to step outside while they spoke in private.

I thought, "Oh my god, what have I done? Have I overstepped my boundaries? Maybe they think I've pushed Alessandro too far." (I was just a volunteer however, so they couldn't fire me.)

I had explained to them that I just wanted to practice what I had been studying because I didn't want to get rusty over the summer. I still had my final year to complete, and I had to do my thesis. I needed to continue with my education and was hoping they could be a resource for me to perhaps do my research there the following September.

I didn't want to alienate anyone. I wanted to make a good impression, and, now, they were discussing me and the work I had done with the boys. I was nervous thinking that I had perhaps made them feel uncomfortable by delving too far into what was personal and confidential.

I waited for what seemed to be about a half hour or so. Finally, they invited me back in.

They told me that they were truly impressed with the level of professionalism they had seen in the few short months I had been working with the boys. Furthermore, they felt I would be an added resource for the boys that, at this time, they felt would be necessary for their mental well-being and development. They wanted to know if I would be available to continue to work there in the fall.

I was stunned. I explained that I had originally asked the organization for a position, but I was told they weren't hiring. I also told them that I had to do my thesis the following year, that I would love to be able to continue with this population, and that I would be honored to do so.

The director said he would talk to the powers that be because he wanted me to be part of their team. I didn't know if he would be able to pull the strings he needed to in order to get me a position but I was excited about the possibility. When I further explained that I hadn't even graduated yet and didn't have a degree, he told me "Don't worry I'll have you work under one of the psychologists as a paid intern."

Now, I was the one standing there with my mouth open. I was totally taken by surprise.

To say that the summer had been a worthwhile adventure would be an understatement. What surprised me the most was the director's determination in getting me to stay! What I didn't know was how big a challenge I would have in front of me. Here was a facility with hundreds of children, and I would be the only art therapist. September would prove to be the most daring experience I had ever been confronted with. I had no idea what I would be up against, but I was ready and willing to find out.

September

$\mathcal{S}$EPTEMBER WAS A TIME of great change for me. I was assigned one house on the campus the same one I worked with over the summer. I was bumped up to twenty-one hours a week, which was perfect since I was also in graduate school. I was on the payroll and finally had access to the boy's files.

Reading their files confirmed a lot of what I was seeing, and gave me more insight. I would now be able to ask the right questions to steer the boys into a greater understanding of their place within their family structures and to help them understand their reactions to that structure (or in many cases, lack of structure).

I was to work directly under a psychologist who had about ten years experience with these boys and who also worked with the same boys I was assigned to. She was very knowledgeable and helpful. Together, we were able to brainstorm ways to approach the boys.

She also helped me decipher the meaning of some of the images the boys were showing me. It wasn't just their artwork that we were looking at but their body language, what they said, and what went unsaid. Sometimes their avoidance told me more about them than if they just told me their entire story.

School was challenging, but what I had to focus on the most was my thesis. Somehow, I had to separate the schoolwork from the workplace. When I was on the campus, I gave the boys my full attention and wrote everything down. I also had to make a case to the board of psychologists there that I had a concrete plan for a nonbiased research project for my thesis. Plus, I had a husband and two teenage daughters of my own who needed a lot of attention; you could say my plate was full.

What I learned to do was be in the moment and focus on the matter at hand. When I was in session with a client that was all I could think about. I had my supervisors at school and at work if I needed help with any situation, I felt I could get my questions answered and confident that I could do a good job.

I continued to see Alessandro. I think he was relieved that I was staying on and that our sessions together would not be interrupted. He couldn't bear any more change in his life, and having one thing be constant was helpful for him.

Now that I was on the staff I was able to review files, I found out Alessandro had a police record from an assault charge presumably issued by his mother and her boyfriend. This is not an uncommon situation; the child doesn't want to accept the replacement "father". He had a strong allegiance to his biological father and his extended family on that side especially his grandfather who he looked up to as his savior; he didn't want a surrogate dad.

This boy had become so stressed from his family's situation that he was hearing voices that told him to start fires. I have come to regard fire setting as a frantic call for help, like a red flag desperately trying to grab someone's attention and say "Help me I'm dying!"

In the fall, Alessandro finally started to talk about his family. Evidently, there was a lot of domestic violence at home, and it seemed as if alcohol was the match that lit the fire (figuratively speaking). I was not in a position to judge anyone, so I just listened to him. What was striking to me was the emotion with which Alessandro relayed his story.

Apparently, as a young boy growing up, he was on his own a lot. His parents were too involved with their own problems to take much notice of him. He never had any money, so when he went to school and got hungry, he would just take what he needed. He then began stealing so that he could buy his lunch.

That evolved into other things like "stealing money for clothes," as Alessandro put it. His sneakers were too small for him, and he couldn't walk to school anymore because they hurt his feet too much, so he felt justified in stealing the money he needed to buy new sneakers.

As time went on, Alessandro said he got so good at stealing that he could pick anyone's pocket anywhere. He would go down to the center of a busy intersection in the city, where he knew there would be a lot of people, and just help himself.

He became known in school as the kid who could get you anything. And so other boys began hiring him to get stuff for them: sneakers, hoodies, cell phones, and so on.

This inflated Alessandro's ego, and he developed a personality around his illegal activity that had all the rewards he needed. He fed himself, dressed himself, and offered rewards to other kids who befriended him. Mind you, he was only about ten years old when this all started, and it continued until the assault charge landed him in a juvenile detention center at age fourteen.

As it turned out, his mother gained custody of her three children, which from all outward appearances didn't go well for Alessandro. It seemed as though she was the type of woman who wanted to be friends with him; she liked to hang out with him and his friends but, unfortunately, it didn't appear as if she could mother him. She was mostly interested in dating and, as Alessandro put it, she brought around some pretty unsavory characters.

Around this same time, Alessandro was having a recurring dream at the (RTC) Residential Treatment Center. He would dream that he was back home in his own bedroom, and it felt so real he thought he was actually there until he woke up and found himself in this home for boys.

I asked Alessandro to draw me a picture of his room. His bed was like on a wave, and the carpet was as big and blue as the ocean. He seemed to be lost in a sea of emotion, drifting along on a raft without a place to anchor him down.

After Alessandro was sent to juvenile detention, his mother's rights to him came into question; evidently, the authorities found evidence of neglect on her part but that would take time to prove meanwhile, all Alessandro could do was wish that his father and grandfather would get custody of him.

Alessandro was also involved in a group project in art therapy, in which the boys were creating an island with all the things they needed to survive on it. Moving along these lines, I decided to ask Alessandro to draw what he was thinking about while on his island.

He said he dreamt about being in his room at his grandfather's house. The picture he drew consisted of himself, his grandfather and his dad. I asked him what was missing from the picture, he said his mom.

The next step was to draw a picture of himself with his mom. He drew her on one side of the paper and put himself all the way on the other side. I said, "It looks as if the two of you are pretty far apart." He said, "yeah, oh yeah, that's the way it has to be for now. I want it that way because I'm still mad at her for pressing charges against me and for placing her boyfriend ahead of me."

He then drew a wall between them, saying that, for now, it would be better to keep his distance from her. He needed time and space to figure things out.

I then asked him to put his dad in the picture, and he placed his father right behind him. This gesture suggested that his dad had his back. Of course the only person missing at this point was his grandfather. Alessandro put him above everyone else, taking up the entire top of the drawing, larger than life. This is how he saw his family. It was very clear who was most important and who was there for him.

What was unclear to me, however, was whether or not his assumptions were accurate. His perspective needed to be honored, but there are always two sides to every story, and all I had was his side. I learned a long time ago that you never take sides in marital disputes. How was I to know if his mother was justified in trying to recreate a new life for herself.

My dilemma was, should I try and repair the relationship between Alessandro and his mother or help him to move on? Wasn't part of my job description to bring the family together? What would my supervisor have to say about it?

Apparently, she was taking the fifth on this one. Dr. Gibson wanted to wait and see how things played out. My understanding about bonding was that it was very hard to break the bond between a mother and child, and most kids, no matter how badly they were rejected or neglected by their mothers, would usually want to stay with them.

That is what made me question this blatant rejection of his mother on Alessandro's part. I had a feeling that there was a male alliance occurring, a silent code between the father, grandfather and son that made it virtually impossible for Alessandro to extend an olive branch to his mother. Was he trying to man up?

At about the same time the weather outside started turning colder I was still working from my car and carrying a lot of art supplies around with me. What I needed was a place to set up shop. I started using the basement of the house where the boys lived but I needed more space.

I made a request for a more permanent office/art room, and they found me a space in another building across campus. Unfortunately, it was another basement. It was a small room but at least it had a sink and some cupboards.

I put in an additional request for some cabinets, a desk, and, of course, some more art supplies. I also got a computer and was linked to the center's system so that I could write my progress notes.

At the time, I was also taking the center's self-defense training program. This was very important because I was a bit cut off from the rest of the world, being down in the basement, and if a problem ever arose, I would need to defend myself.

Nevertheless, I was extremely happy to have a room to work in. It's difficult sometimes, working out of your car because you can only carry around so much stuff, and you never knew what you might need in the middle of a session. If a boy got motivated and wanted to express himself more fully, pencil and paper might not be enough.

Now that I was working more hours and seeing more boys, naturally, I needed a variety of other materials. You never knew what creative outlet a kid would need to express themselves in. It's wonderful to have it all clay, paint, paper, paper maché, all of which could be a messy proposition, so you need to have it along with a sink, glue, flour and water, newspaper and a good amount of space. Needless to say, it is something you need to plan a bit in advance for. I don't like to suggest working in a particular medium and then not be able to deliver.

The room I had was small, about 10' by 12', and was fine for one-on-one sessions but when I had the group it was a bit tight. There was another room in this basement that was like a lounge. It had a couch and some upholstered chairs, and it was carpeted. This room wasn't used that often by the staff, so I used it to process information during groups.

I wasn't in a position to complain so I just dealt with what I had, but I sure could have used a bigger studio to work in. I even sat down and drew a picture of the room I wanted. It was big with windows all around and had a sink and lots of storage space. I hung the picture up in the art room thinking that if I looked at it every day, eventually, I would get a room just like it.

Since most of the boys were not allowed to roam freely on the campus I had to pick them up from the residence I was working with and transport them across campus to my new space. Having to escort them to and fro from each session cut into our time, they had to earn the privilege of having the freedom to walk around campus on their own, so for now I was the designated chaperone.

At this juncture in my work with Alessandro, it seemed to be the time to find out about loyalty and allegiance. In order to do this, I had to be observant and patient, waiting to see what would develop. Alessandro was creative and intelligent; whatever he had in his mind he could represent without a problem.

Without getting too intense, keeping sessions playful, I opted to start making some masks. I had studied about the culture of the Islands and knew that they had a wonderful carnival every year that was celebrated in the streets, with music and dancing. Interestingly enough, they wore these wonderful decorative masks called Caretas, paper maché masks that the *vejigante* (dancers) would wear while dancing in the street.

Alessandro was very proud of his heritage, and he liked the idea of making some masks for himself. They usually had horns on them and scary faces, which were meant to ward off evil spirits. Alessandro worked on his masks for several weeks. He actually made two of them: one had red horns that looked like a little devil and the other one had fangs and a big ugly mouth.

Our sessions became very animated when I asked Alessandro to talk about the pieces. I inquired if the one mask with the mouth could talk what would this mouth say.

"The first one, the one with the teeth," he said, "was as if she were yelling at me." ("She" I thought. "Okay, it's a she.")

"What does she say?" I asked.

"She always yells at me; all the time, she's mean and says things that put me down," he replied.

"You make it sound as if you know this person," I said.

"Oh yeah, I do," said Alessandro. (He didn't say exactly who he was referring to but I assumed he was referring to his mother). "She never takes my side."

"So talk to her; tell her whatever you want."

"Shut up. Stop yelling at me! Stop taking everyone else's side. She never shuts up; she just keeps on yelling and yelling at me."

"Then what happens?" I asked.

"I turn into this." Alessandro pointed to the other mask, the devil mask. "She makes me angry. She makes me turn into this ugly thing, and anyone who gets in my way gets it."

"What do you do when you get like that?"

"I break things, and hit things. You should see my room; it has holes all over the walls."

"Tell her how you feel; tell her that all of her yelling makes you turn into this devil".

Alessandro turned to the mask and yelled, "You're a witch, and you make me so angry! You're the devil, not me. You make me crazy! Why can't you ever take my side in things? You never believe me; you don't care about me."

"Alessandro, I can see that you are really upset, that she makes you feel hurt inside. She is your mother and you expect her to love you.

Alessandro went on to say, "She seems to better deal me for her boyfriends, and uses me to get back at my dad."

"I can see that she really gets to you! You can see that, can't you? I can feel that you are frustrated and hurt."

He was shaking and trembling now. I said "Okay Alessandro, sit down and relax. You told her how you feel; you got it out. You don't have to punch holes in the walls. You don't have to hurt yourself anymore. You're not really like that devil. I never see you get angry with the other boys. You always try and patch things up; you're the peacemaker in the group".

"I don't like getting angry like that," said Alessandro.

"What do you like to do?"

"I like to go to my island," he replied, referring to the island he was making in the group.

"Okay, that's great. Let's go to your island."

"I just want to be alone on my island where no one can bother me."

This was an extraordinary moment, when Alessandro finally addressed the object of his frustration and hurt. It seemed at last, he understood that his mother was not the mother he needed or wanted to have. He wants to be first in her eyes, not last. This was the rub. This is what got him so angry.

He put it all out there on the table; now what was he to do with it? I needed to talk to my supervisor. What would she advise him to do? Should he turn his back on his mother, or should he try and patch things up with her?

When I went to see my supervisor for my weekly visit, I confided in her that I felt for Alessandro and his feelings of being let down by his mother. I was starting to have doubts about whether or not they would be able to repair their relationship.

What she said surprised me because I hadn't thought this way before. She said, often times, the relationship cannot be repaired and shouldn't be repaired, that the relationship might be too toxic, and that Alessandro needed to insulate himself from being further damaged.

I checked the books to make sure and according to the records his mother was MIA. She wasn't attending the court hearings, and she had no contact with the boy since he was put into placement. At this point her rights were being terminated, and the court was looking to place Alessandro with his grandfather.

This shed a whole new light on the direction I would go with him. In my naiveté, I was thinking along an old paradigm, that it was always best to repair the mother-child relationship. I was beginning to learn that it wasn't always in the best interest of the child to try and repair the connection.

I had been working on my thesis during this time, and the theme I was working on was using the traumatic state of dissociation in a positive way. What commonly happens when a child is confronted with terror is that the brain will split off into fragments because the child is too frightened to take it all in. Part of his/her consciousness dissociates in order to protect the psyche from further deterioration. (Herman, 1992). I postulated that if you could use the ability to dissociate in a controlled manner, then the client maybe able to remember the traumatic event and reconstruct it in a positive way.

Judith Herman talks about this in her book, *Trauma and Recovery*. She says that, in the Second World War, in their quest for a quick and effective method of treatment, military psychiatrists discovered the mediating role of altered states of consciousness in psychological trauma. Herman posited that children might also choose to alter their experience by rationalizing a parent's behavior in some way or deleting it from consciousness altogether (Herman, 1992).

Such efforts could lead to denial, a state of trance, or even complete dissociation from reality. These conditions could be highly developed in abused children. As a consequence, dissociation becomes not only a defense mechanism but a basic personality trait (Herman, 1992).

This gave me the idea that dissociation could be used effectively in treating trauma, particularly PTSD. I recognized that Alessandro had all of the symptoms of PTSD; he had nightmares; he was hyper-aroused most of the time, and prone to angry outbursts and depression.

What I wanted to do next was bring Alessandro into an altered state to allow some of his traumatic events to surface. This would allow him to deal with these events release them once and for all. In this way these memories would not keep undermining his efforts to move forward.

In our next session, I used a simple guided imagery to relax Alessandro because I knew from my research that you couldn't be relaxed and anxious at the same time. This is called systematic desensitization, a theory developed by Wolpe.

Wolpe held the notion that what we fear in reality is paralleled in the imagination, thus, that which we no longer fear in the imagination would not disturb us in reality (Wolpe, 1969).

In other words, Alessandro's greatest fear was being abandoned by his mother. That permeated his entire being and was lodged in his memory. And though it might very well be true, as long as it sat there in his memory and imagination, it would continue to plague him.

In the next session, I asked Alessandro when was the first time he really felt angry, like the kind of anger he felt the week before toward his mother. He said he couldn't remember because he had been in a car accident and didn't remember things that well. I knew it was because he had suppressed it so far back in his mind that it was difficult to retrieve. In addition, he might have dissociated during the original event and therefore buried it further.

According to Van der Kolk, there is a whole cascade of events that take place in the brain. When a person becomes overly stressed during times of extreme trauma, there is an increase in cortisol levels leading to more tryptophan to be released in the system. The excess cortisol causes the hippocampus and amygdala to malfunction (Brown, Ebert, & Goyer, 1982 p 742, cited in Van der Kolk, 1988).

Neuroscientists are discovering that this is what the body does as a way of protecting the individual from trauma. The amygdala's primary function is the formation and storage of memories associated with emotional events. The hippocampus stores long-term memory (Van der Kolk, 1988).

During these highly charged emotional events, the endocrine glands secrete such enormous amounts of hormones; the system becomes flooded making these two critical areas shut down. Overtime, neuroscientists have found that the hippocampus becomes atrophied and shrinks down in size causing the general declarative memory to be lost. Overtime, if untreated, this will eventually undermine one's experience for a healthy integrated psyche (Van der Kolk, 1988 p. 276).

"Severe or prolonged stress, accompanies an increase in corticosteroid levels resulting in a suppression in hippocampal functioning and thus amnesia for traumatic experiences" (Squire, 1987, p. 283, cited in Van der Kolk, 1988). Suffice to say that the body protects itself by deliberately forcing certain events to become forgotten by the rational mind.

I used a simple guided imagery technique to help relax Alessandro and bring him back to his childhood. All he had to do was breathe deeply and imagine walking through the woods, all the way back to the house he lived in when he was a child. He went back to a time when he was only five years old.

He was standing in front of his house in the driveway and he could hear his parents inside the house fighting and yelling at each other. Finally, his mother came out of the house, slamming the screen door. She had Alessandro's youngest sister, who was only about two at the time, in her arms.

Her boyfriend was waiting in a car at the end of the driveway, and she ran right to the car, passing by Alessandro as if he wasn't there. She got into the car and drove off. Alessandro was left in the driveway alone, crying for his mother.

"What were you thinking then? Can you remember?" I asked Alessandro.

He said, "I felt let down, lied to, angry, and sad." He also felt that maybe it was his fault because he kept messing up.

"That is the same way you feel now, isn't it?" I asked.

He said, "I'm still angry and sad, and I feel let down."

"What happened after that event?"

He said that he, his older sister, and father got together and decided to give his mother another chance. She came back, but he said she never took care of him. He started to remember a lot of things about that time like a birthday that came and went with no mention, no parties.

His parents were always fighting, and he remembered that one time his father hit his mother. Again, she left, but, this time, pressed charges against the dad. That is when she got custody of the kids.

Things really got bad after that time. Alessandro told me, she didn't do anything to take care of them. She didn't buy them clothes and, a lot of times, there wasn't enough food in the house. That was when he started stealing. The last straw was when her boyfriend came to the house and started yelling at Alessandro, saying he was no good, that his sister was a slut, and that his dad was a bum.

Alessandro lost it at that point and went after the boyfriend with a kitchen knife. That was when he was arrested and sent to a juvenile detention center. Again, he said, he felt the same way: alone, let down, lied to, and angry.

It was times like these that I had to really control myself. I could get caught up in the emotion of what my client was telling me. In my mind, I wanted to cheer for Alessandro that he had the gumption to stand up to this intruder but I had to bite my tongue and just listen.

Of course, you can't settle disagreements with a knife, but I could understand that he was pushed to the breaking point. Why wasn't an investigation done into the family at that point? Instead, Alessandro became the bad guy, even though he was trying to do the right thing by standing up for his sister.

I wanted to go back to the five-year-old boy. How had he messed up? What could he have done at five years of age that could have caused all that trouble? He said he was bad, he didn't listen, he acted up, and he felt that a lot of the time his parents were fighting because of his bad behavior.

I explained to him that it was common for little kids to feel that it was their fault that their parents were fighting; children love their parents so much, they don't want to believe they are bad, so they blame themselves. "I'm not telling you that your parents were bad people, but their fighting had to do with a lot of grown-up things that a little boy couldn't understand," Alessandro just listened.

I also explained that his behavior might have been an attempt to get his parent's attention because they were so preoccupied with their own problems that they weren't thinking about him or taking care of his needs. When I said this, he seemed to have a moment of insight. He just sat there not knowing what to say.

I suggested that he let go of some of the guilt he was hanging on to. I wanted him to remember that he was still a young boy and that he couldn't solve his parent's problems. He looked so sad I wanted to hug him and tell him everything would be alright, but I knew that his family's problems were not going to just disappear and that he couldn't change them. All I could do was help change the way he reacted to his parents and how he perceived them.

What was interesting to note was that the relaxation exercise allowed Alessandro to access most of his repressed emotion and memory of an event that caused him a lot of pain and may have been a turning point in his young life.

I call these moments shut down moments a phrase coined by Roger Wooler. What I have learned to do in these instances, as taught by (Roger Woolger, 1988), is to slow down the event as if you were watching a movie. Review the event in slow motion so you can extract exactly what you were thinking and feeling at the time.

For Alessandro this proved to provide the insight he needed to understand what really happened in that moment and to stop blaming himself for his mother's apparent lack of empathy and caring for him.

Thesis

$\mathcal{S}$CHOOL WAS STARTING AGAIN and I had to work on my thesis. But before I could do anything I had to convince the clinical director at the center that I had a worthwhile project and ask her permission to conduct my study there. What I wanted to do was use guided imagery and art therapy together as a way to reduce depression and disruptive behavior in adolescent boys.

I had prepared a demonstration of how art therapy worked. My premise was that guided imagery would help reduce resistance in retrieving traumatic information by relaxing the client long enough to allow the images to emerge from the subconscious; bypassing their usual defense mechanisms. Mental pictures relating to their trauma would be brought up and drawn in art therapy, then discussed and transferred back into the conscious mind. This way the information would be cognitively understood and transformed into manageable bits that could be integrated back into the psyche.

This was a tall order since these psychologists weren't familiar with art therapy let alone guided imagery. I was treading on new territory so I had to be convincing. I showed them art produced by some of the boys I had worked with in the past and explained how the whole thing came about.

They seemed interested but said that, in order for the results to be untainted, I would need to work with boys I hadn't worked with before, and they would need to be freed to be in a study. Basically, what they were telling me was that I had to find boys who would be willing to be part of a study and who were wards of the state so the agency could sign off on them. This made sense to me because most of the parents were not that involved with their children and they would be very difficult to contact. If the kids were under eighteen their parents would have to sign off for them, but if they were wards of the state the agency could sign off for them and give them permission.

On a campus with hundreds of children, I had to interview dozens of kids in order to find just those few who would be interested. And I was not able to persuade them in any way, as a so called bribe or reward system could taint the results. I was told to talk to the woman in charge of the research department as she could give me a list of boys whose parents had given up their rights to them.

This made me hopeful, and so I met with the researcher on the campus. Her name was Annie, and she wasn't particularly happy to see me. She was terse and treated me with disdain as if she didn't have time, making it very clear she wasn't interested in my research.

On the other hand, I made friends with Mary, the secretary in that department. She was a breath of fresh air we seemed to have a lot in common. Mary had been with the agency for many years, and she knew everything that was going on. We had a lunch date set up so that we could talk freely with no time restraints, and she gave me an ear full.

Evidently, the budget for the research department had been cut and cut, and then cut some more, and a staff of four people had been reduced to just this one woman. She was overworked and underpaid, and no one in the agency was interested in what she was doing.

It was an uphill battle for her and I could understand how she felt. Apparently, ever since this new CEO had taken charge of the agency, she had become obsolete. The new director was interested in getting government funding and grants, and apparently, there was no money available for research so her budget was cut, the direction changed on how the agency would function.

Money was available for job placement training, higher education, special education for boys in placement, and sports. There were some great athletes on the campus, and a lot of the agency's money was spent on sports programs. I thought all of these programs were worthwhile, but that research was also important. However, they couldn't get funding for it, so it was being phased out.

Proceeding with the study meant I had my work cut out for me and no one to help. I got a list of all the boys who were freed by the courts and started interviewing them. I had to again introduce myself to their social workers and explain what I was doing, and then ask them if they had time to meet with me.

That was like asking God to make more time because what I was finding out was that most of the people on this campus were overworked and underpaid. To put one more thing on anyone's plate would not be fair or popular.

Everyone's schedule was different, and the children were all kept busy. They had school, tutors, reading programs, sports, jobs, training programs, and so on. It was taking me months to get it all worked out, and I had to have each boy who would be in the program sign off on it, as well as their social workers. Then I had to find a time for weekly group sessions that would work for everyone involved. I felt as if I was running a marathon, and I was getting worried that time would run out for me to complete the research by the end of the semester.

The research was to be conducted over an eight week period. I had an experimental group who would receive art therapy and guided imagery every week for eight weeks, and a similar control group who would receive the same program for eight weeks, but without the guided imagery. All of the participants had to show up every week consistently for the entire eight weeks in order for the study to work.

However, kids are very unpredictable, especially kids with emotional problems. How I was going to keep them interested would be challenging, all I could do was take each day as it came and keep my eye on the end goal, I managed t¢ to pull it together logistically. I got six boys to volunteer, and three were randomly put into either the control group or the experimental group. I also had to pre-test and post-test them.

I wanted to use an instrument that would test their level of trauma, but I was told that the boys were in no way to be alarmed or made to feel re-traumatized. I also wanted to test their level of creativity, but my department chair said that was impossible; no one could be tested for that. I had ordered the Torrance Test for creative thinking, but my supervisor at work wouldn't accept it as a valid instrument.

My theory was that if I could break through their defense mechanism, it would free them up psychologically then they would naturally become more creative. If I could determine what their level of creativity was at the onset, then I could test their level again in the end of the eight weeks to see if their level of creativity increased.

I had to think outside of the box, be more imaginative myself in order to figure out a way to measure their creative impulses. I found an instrument that I could use called FEATS or the Formal Elements of Art Therapy Scale (Gantt & Tabone, 1990; 1993). In this instrument, there was a rector scale that could measure things like prominence of color, implied energy, the amount of space used, and the amount of details used in a drawing. This would offer quantitative numeric data to substantiate my findings.

I would pretest the boys in each group by asking them to draw a person picking an apple from a tree. Then, at the end of the eight weeks of intervention, I would ask them to draw the same thing and have the two drawings compared by an independent third party rater.

I hypothesized that the residents receiving eight weeks of art therapy and guided imagery would have a significant reduction in depression; their disruptive behaviors would drop, they would use more color in their drawings; they would effectively show more energy in their drawings, and there would be an increase in the amount of details in the drawings.

I realized that these changes could happen because of saturation, meaning drawing more often would affect the internal reliability; but both groups were exposed to drawing in the same way, so there was consistency in the measurement. There would be an increase in creative endeavors because of exposure and because they wouldn't be as depressed as they were before the intervention, simply due to the fact that they were addressing some of their core issues.

I also felt that the guided imagery would loosen up the stronghold that their psyche had on them; releasing the imagery related to their trauma would change their awareness with regard to their imposed amnesia to the past. Within the safety of the art room, they could deal with the suppressed information, bring it up to the light of day, look at it for what it was, deal with it once and for all, and put it behind them in the past where it belonged, where it would no longer plague them and bring them down, physically, emotionally, intellectually and psychologically.

I was certain that it would work because I had done it for myself, and I knew that it could be done for them. I had been haunted by a traumatic childhood fraught with sickness and a totally dysfunctional family. However, I used guided imagery and art to unleash my suppressed memories, and I was sure I could do it for them. All I had to do was prove it.

Now back at the Research Department; they gave me a list of possible behaviors that could be rated before the intervention and after in order to record stability overtime. This list consisted of everything from not washing themselves, physical outbursts to setting fires. The list was divided into three groups: not so serious, moderately serious, and very serious/bizarre.

I charted the boys' behaviors for a month before the intervention and for a month after the intervention by reviewing the logbook from their houses and the behavior incident reports. It was a daunting task to read this pile of papers prepared for each boy and then track it for a month before I started seeing them, during the intervention, and for a month after I finished working with them. Nevertheless, it was important to document because I wanted to see if the results would be sustained over a long period of time, if not permanently, as a significant change in behavior.

The behaviors were added up and made into a graph so I would be able to substantiate my results. Numbers don't lie, and that was the key to the success of the research, but it would take time, and I was supposed to have this study completed by April.

I had no life during this period. All I did was research, read, and work. It was a hard time. I was chained to the computer, my husband was fed up with me, and, with what little time I did have, I was running to parent–teacher conferences, working on proms, organizing trips for my own kids, and trying to find time to spend weekends in the country to try and relax. Not the easiest thing to do, as I was anything but relaxed.

If I didn't have to go to school and do this insane research, life would be easy, but you couldn't get a master's degree without a thesis project. Plus, I couldn't get an art therapy license if I didn't have a master's degree. And who would hire me without a degree? As it was, I was working as an intern, and I couldn't keep that status forever. I just had to keep my head up and keep on going.

I did some of my own visualizations around this time and drew myself with my diploma in hand, rising up above all of the books and papers, as if I was climbing Mount Everest. I kept telling myself, "Keep your eye on the prize; keep going. Put one foot in front of the other, and just keep on moving in the right direction. Eventually, you will get there."

I couldn't believe all of the people who had dropped out of my program since the thesis research started. Some artists are into their own process, and it is very difficult for them to shift gears and suddenly start doing research. I actually didn't mind the reading and the research. I have always enjoyed learning new things.

What I found most difficult was learning the (APA) American Psychological Association style of writing. Everything had to be documented a certain way. For me, that was the most challenging thing I had ever done.

You have to have a scientific mind for this sort of thing. I am a color, texture, shape, line kind of visual thinker, and I just couldn't wrap my brain around notations, quotes, and referencing. I was beginning to think that getting my master's degree was an endurance test. If you could survive the drill you got the credential.

Going Full Circle

*Y*OU ARE PROBABLY WONDERING why I wanted to use guided imagery as a means to unraveling the trauma complex. When I was working at one of my first internships, I came in contact with a young girl whose biological age was seventeen, but her maturity level was more like a young five or six year old.

I knew that she was regressed because of some trauma and I could see in her drawn images and symbols that she had been sexually abused, the drawings confirmed my suspicions, even though it had not been documented in her chart history. What her chart did indicate was that she had suicidal ideation; she acted out sexually and she was very depressed. That behavior is characteristic of this type of trauma, and I wanted to find out the root cause. The agency should have tried to identify what had caused her diagnosis, but they had no evidence, so no formal charges were ever filed, they could not press charges or bring a case to court, without proof.

In my dealings with Young Girl, known for now as (YG) I was shown what dissociation was all about. What I observed in session was remarkable and note worthy.

She had recently taken a long trip to one of the Caribbean Islands with her dad to visit his family. Evidently, it was a fabulous trip, and it was all she could talk about, she wanted to make a book documenting it. She worked on it for several weeks and said she was finished with it when I noticed she hadn't drawn a picture of her dad who was the one she went with to visit "his" family. So I asked her if she would like to include a picture of the two of them together on the trip. She said okay.

She started the drawing the same as most of her other drawings of three rain clouds in the sky with rain drops coming down. Then she started a very childlike line drawing of the two of them when, all of a sudden she went into a catatonic state, (which is a condition of complete trance). She stayed that way for quite some time with her hand suspended in mid air.

I had never seen anything like this; I kept calling her name until she finally came out of it. When I asked her if she was all right, she snapped at me saying, "You know I'm depressed; I take medication for it."

"Yes," I said, "is there something about this particular drawing that made you upset?" She said, "I miss my cousins. That's all; I miss them, and it makes me sad."

That was a good cover-up but I knew there was more to the story that she wasn't telling me. It became quite clear to me that she had been abused by her father since an early age, and she just couldn't speak about it, either because of fear of him hurting her further or because her father had made her so dependent on him that she didn't know how to function without him, and she didn't want him being sent away.

I had never seen anything quite like this before and documented it. In time, when I had enough evidence to present to the board, I called a special meeting to discuss her case.

I wanted the agency to press charges against the father and use her drawings as evidence, but, unless she admitted some wrongdoing, that was never going to happen. I had quite an extensive file of drawings that by any analysis would have substantiated my assessment.

In a few short months YG was turning eighteen, and she was eligible to sign herself out of care and move back home with her parents. I had wanted her to be discharged to a group home with other sexually abused girls so that she could find support with the other girls and, perhaps in time, be able to discuss what happened to her.

Her father was adamant about her coming home, and he wouldn't sign the papers needed to send her to a group home, he had complete control over her. I was extremely frustrated, but, no matter how I tried to get YG to talk about her childhood, she would inevitably put the brakes on. All I could do was be in the moment with her and try to ground her and build up her self esteem. This case study brought me face to face with how devastating dissociation can be.

I knew about dissociation from my studies, and I had known about it all along from my own childhood. If I really thought hard about it, I could probably pin point the first time I dissociated. I believe it was when I was about three years old.

I was a patient at Columbia Presbyterian Hospital in NY, and I was in critical condition. I had been diagnosed with neuphrosis, a kidney disease which caused my system to become very toxic with its own waste. I had peritonitis, pneumonia, along with very high fevers.

This one particular episode, the doctors had packed me in a tub of ice-cold water to bring my fever down. When I was back in my bed my mother was at my bed side saying the rosary, and a priest had been called in to give me extreme unction or last rites. I believe, during that time, I was delirious and out of my body for most of it. I can remember looking back down at the tub and watching the whole experience unfold.

This picture was taken of me when I was about 3 at the height of my illness. I was swollen from the fluid that would build up in my system and from the medications they gave me.

Many years later I actually painted a picture of a similar experience when another priest had been called in when I was in my hospital bed with an extremely high fever. I had the feeling that there was an Angelic presence in the room that was protecting me, with my mom at my side. All totaled, I had been given last rites three times. Each time I believe I had dissociated.

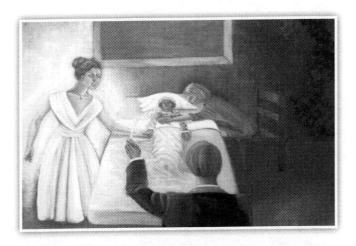

Oil painting by De Pietro called "Last Rites"

In between my stays at the hospital, I would go home to my family. The funny thing was that going home was not what I wanted; as a matter of fact, I preferred being in the hospital because, I knew at least there, I would be safe.

There was a tremendous amount of arguing and fighting going on between my parents, making going home a frightening experience. Whenever they would fight, I would tune out, mentally, that is. I didn't know what it was at the time. It just happened all by itself, but, trust me, it helped me get though the tough times.

As long as my mom was there, I felt there was a buffer between myself and the monster my (dad). My dad would go into these tirades with no warning. When he went off, he couldn't stop himself. It would escalate until my mom would end up getting hurt.

I would either run and hide in my room or dissociate. I wanted to be invisible so he wouldn't see me and come after me and hurt me. You would never know what would set him off. For example, if dinner was late or the food was cold or if dinner was something out of a can and not homemade, he would have a fit and then he would start to rev up. One thing would lead to another, and there was no telling where it would end up.

If I or anyone else ever uttered one word in rebuttal, it would just add fuel to the fire. He would eventually tire himself out, but not until something got broken, like dishes, chairs, or my mother's heart. The next day, he would be remorseful and try and be nice to everyone. He would try and make up by taking us out to dinner, or buy my mother a mink coat or something. It was such an emotional roller coaster.

When my brother and sister got a little bit older and more rebellious, he would turn his temper tantrums on them. He would beat them as badly as he beat my mother, but for some reason, he never beat me. I kept my head down, my mouth shut, and tried to stay out of his way. I also think, maybe because I was so sickly as a child, he thought it was better to leave me alone.

It's no wonder I chose to study psychology later on in life; I had a need to try and understand my dad. One minute, he was Mr. nice guy, the most generous and giving person in the world, and, the next, he was like the devil himself. He was all about power and control.

I came to this understanding during my psychological studies that he was what is known, as a classic borderline personality. To this day, I have a hard time working with borderline personality clients. I have to refer them out because they trigger me way too much.

You could never win an argument with my dad. He was always right, and you could never please him either. He was so critical of whatever you did because he had to be the shining star, never anyone else.

He would run very hot, or very cold; everything was either black or white. If he liked you, you could do no wrong, but if you crossed him, he would try to destroy you. He was very vindictive never forgetting anything, and he would hold a grudge.

He was also very cunning the way most predators are, that was why it was so hard to win an argument with him. He would remember everything you said and then use your own words against you and twist their meaning. He was what I would call a master manipulator.

He was also a narcissist, and could talk about himself for hours telling you how great he was, like what a great athlete and friend to his teammates he was. He demanded all of the attention in the room, and if you ever laughed at him or interrupted his story, he would become infuriated.

He probably would have been a great actor. Of course, he had to marry the most beautiful woman in the county. She was stunning, like Rita Hayworth, gorgeous, sweet, and unassuming and a very private person. My mom was his arm candy, and he would show her off every chance he got, and, believe me when I say, he had plenty of opportunities. He was involved in local politics and would parade her around at functions, as every good aspiring politician does.

The problem was that other men were attracted to her as well, and if she ever paid them any attention, she would have to pay a high price for it. My dad was a jealous man, and he kept my mom on a tight leash.

I believe most of the arguments they had were started out of a jealous rage. She could never win; if she was friendly and outgoing, she would have to justify her every action, if she didn't go to functions with him he would get angry with her. She wasn't allowed to work or even go out with her girlfriends. She was trapped.

I don't know how she managed to get through those days. They were hard on all of us but were hardest on her. She loved to go to parties or to host parties it was her coping mechanism; it helped her to forget somehow. In the '50s and '60s there was no shortage of functions for them to attend giving her numerous opportunities to socialize.

Toward the middle of the '60s, my mom suffered a nervous breakdown and had to be hospitalized. That was a tough time for all of us. I think, after she recovered from that episode, she began to plan her escape. She knew that the good times could never out way the bad and as she said to me many times, "I can't live a lie".

I admire her greatly for that, and love her even more now because she showed me that you eventually have to stand up for yourself. She had a small household allowance that she started to put aside in a private bank account, just a little at a time so she wouldn't get discovered. She never told anyone about it. Then she waited for the right opportunity to leave.

In those days there was nowhere for a woman to go get help. It was taboo to discuss family matters outside of the home, not even her own brothers and sisters knew what she was dealing with on a daily basis. There was no shelter or safe house to go to, no family counseling. She was totally on her own.

To anyone else looking at us from the outside, we were the model family; with two cars in the garage, we lived in big house, we had a housekeeper, and we all went to private school. Who could ask for more? No one ever knew the hell we were all living through.

I remember coming home from college during spring break. It was in the early 70's. My mom told me she was leaving, and that she couldn't tell me where she was going.

I couldn't believe my ears "What?" I said "How will I find you?" She said, "When it's safe, I'll get in touch with you." I watched her leave, I never cried so hard.

She got away while my dad was at work. She packed what she could and left. Both my brother and sister were out of the house. I was home alone with the monster.

I had to endure his inquisition. Where did she go? How could you let her go? Why didn't you call me? On and on he went drilling me, like it was my fault. I was terrified of him, yet he acted like a baby.

He couldn't believe that she would leave him. He had never actually entertained the idea that she would go. He had threatened her so many times, beat her so many time and yet she always stayed; he didn't believe she would have the nerve to actually leave.

He was in shock when it finally sank in that she was gone. He absolutely fell apart. He ranted and raved, cried and carried on like I had never seen him do in all of my years of living under his roof. This was something very different.

A few weeks later he tried to commit suicide. I found myself comforting him saying, "She'll be back. You'll see." I was just trying to survive while I was home from school. I couldn't wait to go back to my college campus; I felt so, defenseless.

He tried to boss me around telling me to make him his meals and things like that. I was a nervous wreck, I couldn't wait to leave. Back at school, it was hard to concentrate, but it was only a few months until I would be home for the summer. What in the world was I going to do?

I had nowhere else to go. When I finally arrived home, the house I had grown up in was not my home anymore. It had become a bachelor's pad for all of my dad's friends.

Total strangers were sleeping in my bed, so I had to sleep on the couch. There were nightly card games that lasted until well into the wee hours of the morning, with high stake betting going on by very sleazy characters that were constantly coming and going. He was friendly with underworld, Mafia people, and when I tell you they scared the hell out of me I'm not kidding!

I remember one night very clearly. My dad was screaming on the phone the way he used to yell at my mom, and for some reason, I thought he was talking to her. I don't know whatever possessed me to do this, but I didn't want him to talk to my mom like that anymore. I wanted to protect her. She was free, and I wanted her to stay that way. So I picked up the other phone extension in the house and said, "Stop talking to my mom like that. Stop it". At that point, he dropped the phone and came running down the hall after me yelling, "You little bitch, who do you think you are, telling me what to do?"

He grabbed me and started shaking me. At that point I know I dissociated. The dreaded monster who I had tried to hide from all of my life had finally caught me. I thought he was going to kill me.

He had his hands around my neck and was choking me. I was turning blue when one of his friends came up behind him and grabbed his arms and said, "What are you doing? You're going to kill her." And he pulled his hands off of my throat.

I fell to the floor gasping for air. They left me there while his friend talked to him saying, "She's just a kid. Let her go. She doesn't know anything."

After what seemed to be a long time on the floor, I finally got myself together and grabbed a few things from my room and ran out the door. I was shaking as I jumped into my car and sped off.

I had no idea where I would go. I started living in my car and waited until I could get in touch with some friends. These were the days before cell phones; I had to wait until I could find someone who I thought could help me, and, eventually, an old friend took me into his house until I could sort things out.

What I later found out was that my dad had hired a private investigator to find my mother, and that was the man he was yelling at on the phone. I knew if I went to find her, he would follow me so I had to stay away. I was on my own. It was going to be a long summer.

Eventually, I got in touch with my dad by phone. He was very apologetic, but I would not be in the same room with him alone. I started college again that fall and went to the School of Visual Arts in the city. I got an apartment in the city and stayed away from him as much as I could. Our relationship was very different after that, and I kept my distance. He stopped trying to use me to get to my mother. I didn't see her and I didn't talk to him if I could help it.

She eventually hired an attorney, who tried to negotiate a meeting. I told her not to go, but she felt that maybe he had changed. She met with him one last time in what started off as a reconciliation talk. The meeting went haywire, and in the end, he beat her so badly he nearly killed her.

That is when she knew the relationship could never be rectified; she filed for divorce. I was happy knowing that she was going to finally be safe and away from him.

She got a job doing statistical research for the American Cancer Society. She traveled quite a bit so I never really knew where she was. That was how she kept safe. She stayed on the move. I didn't see her that much after the divorce. It seemed like years.

One thing was for sure; I had learned how to dissociate, and as time went on, I learned how to control it. I used to practice it so that I could manage it. I started to research this phenomenon and found out there was an actual name for it.

They called it "astral projection." I felt more in control when I could do it when I wanted to rather than being triggered by an event into it.

When that happened I had no control. I guess what I was learning was how to be in command of my own emotions so I could distinguish what kind of events would cause me to dissociate. Once you can figure out the kind of things that cause you to dissociate, you can train yourself to recognize the stimuli that cause you to shut down.

Later on, during my own therapy, I learned about triggers and how they worked, I learned how to distinguish triggers and develop coping skills, but this was years before I had any formal training. At this point I was learning how to survive in my own way.

I remember, for example when I was in grade school, a typical trigger for me to dissociate would be, if the teacher was yelling at a student to behave. If it led to a confrontation, my consciousness would be somewhere outside the window. The teacher would then be calling on me, and I would have no idea where we were, or what she was asking of me. Then she would start reprimanding me for not participating properly in class and the cycle would start all over again. If anyone ever raised their voice, especially if it was directed toward me, it would be a trigger.

I became the quintessential escape artist. Speaking of being an artist that was one thing my dad did for me. I begged him for a little space in the basement that I could call my own, my room where I would go and spend hours drawing and painting.

This was my safe place. I spent hours there in my own world, a fantasy world I had to myself, and I loved it. My parents would be upstairs fighting, and I didn't care because I could shut them out and create the world I wanted.

I had originally been introduced to the arts at the Columbia Presbyterian Hospital at their child life center. I think it was the inception of the Child Life Center there. It wasn't anything formal just a few nurses who got together to offer a respite for the kids in care.

I couldn't wait to go down to the art room. We used tongue depressors for spreading paste around and little soufflé cups for putting the paste in. Anything that they had readily available became grist for the creative mill. Anything was better than lying in bed all day feeling sick. This was where we could be kids again and have fun.

As a matter of fact, I did a volunteer position there some forty years later, working in the very same center. I couldn't believe how much it had remained the same. I worked in the oncology unit and brought art supplies right to the bedside of some of the kids who were too sick to get up.

I loved that job, especially when I would appear at the door to their room with the art supply cart and ask if they wanted to play. To see their faces light up was such an inspiration.

A New Challenge: Shane

$\mathcal{M}$Y SUPERVISOR, DR. GIBSON called me down to her office one morning. She said she had something important to ask me. I couldn't imagine what was on her mind, so I didn't even try to speculate.

She said she had a boy she wanted to refer to me. She said he had been with the agency since he was five years old. He was about fifteen now, so he had lived there for the past ten years.

Dr. Gibson admitted to me that they had tried everything with him, and no one seemed to be able to reach him. He had tried to commit suicide three different times. He was depressed, angry, and seemed to be retreating more and more into his own world, making it increasingly more difficult to reach him. This sounded familiar. Shane had one interest, and that was drawing, so Dr. Gibson thought that maybe, just maybe, I could help him through art therapy.

I was surprised at first but realized that most of the kids I worked with fell outside of the realm of textbook cases. I seemed to work with the kids who no one else could help. The more time I spent working in the field of art therapy I realized that art was one modality that could reach people that were difficult to treat with regular talk therapy. And, so I made an appointment to meet with Shane.

Shane appeared to be self-conscious and introverted. He was a tall, blond, blue-eyed young man who wore a T-shirt, hoodie and jeans. He couldn't look at me and kept his head down. When I asked him a question he would mumble back a nondescript answer.

He said he liked to draw, so I showed him the art supplies and asked him which material he liked to work with. He said he usually worked with just pencil and paper. Since all of the boys went to school on the campus, he had limited exposure to the outside world. I don't think he had ever gone to a museum show or gallery exhibit. He did, however, have art in school, and, of course, that was his favorite subject. He wasn't big on sports, as most of the boys on campus were. He mostly stayed to himself and drew on little scraps of paper that he found.

I had a chance to look up his records and found a huge file. You could imagine, after ten years, he had accumulated quite a paper trail. Evidently, his father had died when he was a preschooler, and since his mother had a physical disability, she couldn't take care of him by herself. He was placed in foster care when he was around five but he still had visitation rights with his mom. She had attended parenting classes but was not yet ready to take Shane back home full-time.

I also saw in the folder that his father had died homeless in one of the city parks, having frozen to death. It had never occurred to me that the guy you see begging in the street actually could have a family, wife, kid, and home. It broke my heart to think that this boy had been robbed of a family because of his father's alleged alcoholism.

I was surprised by Shane's inability to articulate his thoughts to me. He was disheveled and seemed to not care about anything, not even himself. I had difficulty in communicating with him and couldn't seem to get him motivated.

After several unremarkable sessions, I began to think that he was mentally challenged as well. But Dr. Gibson had never mentioned that. I had to go and look at his chart again. All I could find was that his IQ was a low normal.

Yet he was so out of it; his face was droopy; he was physically withdrawn and he was physically slouched over, he even sometimes was drooling. I realized he was heavily medicated, and I wondered how I would find the real Shane.

I had some reference books in the art room, so I started to talk to him about art. I spoke to him about art history and the life and times of some of the greatest artists. He seemed interested, but it wasn't enough to get him motivated.

One of the first drawings he ever did in session with me was of a house, a garden, and a tree. His house was very chaotic: broken up shapes for windows like stained glass with lots of geometric shapes that made the building look as if it was broken into pieces. There was a path leading up to the house, but it was irregular, jagged, broken. The house was also up a hill and far away in the distance. It seemed difficult to ever reach the front door. You would have to be somewhat determined to travel it.

Shane put himself in the picture, as an emaciated stick figure working in a garden, which only had a few flowers. In the foreground was a pool of water with a rubber ducky in it. The tree drawn in the yard was hollow and empty looking.

This seemed to represent the little to no nurturing that he had received in his childhood. In the sky was a very sad looking sun with a long droopy face. The stick figure was a stark contrast to the superhero figures he was prone to drawing. And so I asked him, if he wasn't Mr. Universe, who would he be?

Since drawing was the best way Shane could communicate, he drew another picture. In this picture he drew an emaciated man with his ribs sticking out, in a hospital, wearing a hospital gown, and hanging onto an intravenous stand for support. It was clear to me at this point that he did not want to be defined by a physical disability. His greatest fear was to wind up dependant and sickly.

One day, Shane came to session and asked me if I was an artist. I said, "Yes, in fact, I am a gallery painter," and then I had to explain to him where it was that artists would show their work. I then asked him if he would like to see some of my paintings. This seemed to wet his appetite so I showed him my web site.

He didn't say much but sort of got misty eyed. He said "You're really good. You're a real artist," as if he had never met an artist before. I was flattered by the compliment since no one on the entire campus had ever asked me about whether or not I was a painter. It was nice to be able to share my work with someone who had an interest in art. But I think this may have been too threatening to Shane, as he had no idea how one became accomplished in the field.

After that day, the next few sessions became even more labored, and Shane seemed to sink even more into his reclusive self. He even cancelled some sessions altogether. Thinking that I had made a connection with him through the artwork seemed to backfire, and I was at a loss of what to do next. I finally realized that he was intimidated by my experience and technical ability, and so I devised a plan.

One day when Shane came in, he retreated as usual, and I said, "You know what, why don't I draw you? You don't have to do anything but relax, and I'll do your portrait. He said, "Really, you can do that?" I said, "It might not be perfect but I'll give it a try."

And so as I worked, I explained to him everything that I was doing. I showed him things like the simple oval shape for his head to start with, how lightly I would hold the pencil so as to just get the placement and tilt of his head, how the eyes were about a third of the way down in the oval, and how you could divide the oval into thirds for the placement of the eyes, nose, and mouth.

As I did this, he was careening his head around to see everything I was doing. He was mesmerized by the process. I continued with the tutorial until I had the entire head and face mapped out. In the end, I showed it to him and he loved it. I suggested that he finish the drawing with whatever shading or detail he wanted.

In this session he went over his time and I had to finally ask him to leave. He wanted to sign the drawing and take it back to his housemates for all of them to see. I was so pleased that I had finally engaged him into something meaningful.

I realized that he had been intimidated by me and that he was petrified to try and draw in front of me. He had only the slightest bit of confidence, and it hinged on his being able to draw. It was his last bit of hope.

If he suddenly discovered that he couldn't draw, he would have been so devastated that he might have gone off the deep end and really done something to hurt himself; after all, he had made three attempts already. I was finally making a connection with him but I knew I had to be careful. If I pushed too hard or said the wrong thing I would lose him forever. I felt like I was walking on a tightrope.

The next few sessions all went the same way: I would start a drawing, and he would finish it. I would be giving him instruction all along the way, and, to be honest, the boy had talent. He had an innate ability. He just didn't believe in himself.

Every session was full of praise, and, each time, he would take more and more initiative with his drawing. Little by little, he became more independent. After a few months of my starting the drawing and Shane finishing it, he started to draw more on his own. He would go to the library and get reference material and bring it with him to session.

His focus was mostly superheroes, big muscle men that could conquer the world. It became evident that he desperately wanted to connect with his superhero for fear if he didn't he would become weak and unable to take care of himself.

Around this time, I asked Shane to draw me a timeline. He drew an infant and then went right to a teenager with no pictures or important dates in between. He seemed to block out most of his childhood. When I asked him about it, he said he had been in foster care most of his life. He went on to tell me that his mom and stepdad were disabled and couldn't take care of him. His timeline dealt more with his future than his past. He saw himself with a good job and family in the future. He said he wanted to take care of his mom and step dad when he got older.

After about two months of drawing, he was back on track doing most the drawings himself. He only turned to me if he needed help with perspective or some technical detail. I started to notice that he was carrying a folder with him. He was drawing all the time now, and he would carry his drawings around with him.

The other kids in the house were starting to call him "the artist," and he was thriving on the recognition it gave him. He was also starting to look different. He was washing more, he didn't hide inside his hoodie as much, and he would actually look at me while engaged in conversation.

Meeting Lamar

$\mathcal{N}$OT ALL OF THE boys in the house came to art therapy. I had four of them in a group, which started pretty much from the very beginning when I was a volunteer. There was a young boy of only eleven in the group, the youngest in the unit. His name was Lamar; he was hyper and outspoken for his young age. His short time on this planet did not insulate him from having a horrific life experience.

The group was designed to get the boys talking to each other in a constructive way, not the way they were used to. Mostly, they taunted each other, called each other names, and were basically suspicious of each other. Despite this dynamic, Lamar looked up to Alessandro, who was like a big brother to him.

The assignment I proposed over the summer was to design a 3D island that they had all been shipwrecked on. Each boy was to create his own life skill on the island that would assure their survival but that had to be used in cooperation with each other in order to be rescued.

Alessandro had chosen to sleep all day on the imaginary island and be the night watchman; he felt that he was better able to keep everyone safe by patrolling the beach at night. This also kept him separate from everyone else, as he did not want to get to close to anyone, plus he didn't sleep well at night anyway so it served a dual purpose.

Lamar was very bright and creative; he was the toolmaker of the group. He made fishing utensils, fishing nets with fibers he found on the beach, and all sorts of ingenious things. In addition, he was a hunter at night. I could tell that he was a real survivor.

The boys were cooperative and really worked together to make their island. There was a cave for hiding materials in and for sleeping in at night, and a fire pit for keeping warm, cooking, and for keeping wild animals away. They built all kinds of tools out of clay, and they also sculpted the actual island out using sand, incorporating a pond for fresh water for drinking and fishing. They also made a path that led to the beach where there was a dock and a hill that served as a lookout post. There was also a wooded area for hunting, as both Lamar and another boy wanted to be hunters. The island project was turning out to be an exercise in working towards a common goal: survival.

It soon became evident that Lamar and Alessandro had a common bond. While processing the island experience, an amazing discovery unfolded. Most of the time, the boys were very reluctant to talk about personal experiences, but after having worked on the island project together, these two were able to let their guard down just a little.

One day, in the beginning of the fall a conversation started when I inquired about why they chose the jobs they did on the island. Alessandro said he was used to keeping watch during the night because he had lived in the streets, and had to survive out there on his own. Lamar couldn't believe his ears, and admitted that he too had survived on the streets, rummaging for food and trying to get money. The two boys jumped up and hugged each other and said, "Hey, man, I didn't know you were out there like that." There was an instant connection between the two, a shared experience of having been out there on their own without anyone to help them.

I was amazed at how little they really knew about each other; after having lived together for almost a year, they knew nothing about their experiences on the outside. They were even able to find humor in some of their experiences, such as where they hung out, who they knew, running from the cops, hiding, and finding other kids out there that they could trust, and so on.

I was amazed at the depth of knowledge they each had on how to survive out on the streets.

Lamar was only eleven when he came to us as opposed to Alessandro who was fourteen. Lamar was the kind of kid you wanted to protect. I can remember going to his house one day to pick him up for session, when I got there I found out he had locked himself in the bathroom, screaming and crying for his mother, to the point of exhaustion. He screamed "I just want to see her! Why can't I see her?" It broke my heart; how can you tell a kid that his mother was having too hard of a time to have him, that being with her was too dangerous and he was safer here with us?

That's not what they want to here. They want you to tell them that their mothers have been saved, that they have miraculously seen the light and the error of their ways and have now come to their senses and want their baby back.

If only that was the real world. How many times had his mother been in and out of rehab, incarcerated for drug dealing, and still continued to go back to her drug-induced hypnotic state? I thought Alessandro had difficulty in trusting, but Lamar had PTSD, to an even greater degree.

Anything and everything seemed to trigger defensive impulses in Lamar. You never knew what would set him off. One day, in group the boys were cutting out pictures for a collage, and one of the boys went behind Lamar's back and cut a small piece of his hair.

I had to call security to calm him down. It was just a joke but Lamar went into such a tirade. He felt threatened, and under attack. He couldn't calm himself down and had to be restrained. I found out that anything that had to do with knives or sharp objects was a trigger for him. I had looked over the logbook and found that he seemed to be restrained a least once a week. You never knew what would set him off.

After working with him for several years I learned why he reacted the way that he did. He needed to build a safety net around himself that he could feel protected in. He couldn't function in a world that had too much stimuli in it that appeared to be threatening. He had no filter; all he knew was that he had to protect himself.

That's why it was so great for him to make the connection with Alessandro. I can remember commenting to him, "You see, you're not the only one out there feeling alone and vulnerable. There are a lot of kids living in the streets with similar experiences. Wouldn't it be nice for you two to develop a friendship, so that you could learn to be there for each other?" I realized that most of our gangs today are made up of kids just like this who were looking for a safe haven.

Lamar had serious post traumatic stress. It was as if he was still in shock from all the abuse he had sustained as a child. In spite of all of this, he desperately wanted to be reunited with his birth mother. In his mind, he felt somehow responsible for her failures.

When he was finally referred to individual art therapy sessions, he was at long last able to relax. The one-on-one sessions proved to be very therapeutic for him. He couldn't get enough of the individualized attention and soaked it up like a sponge. He looked forward to our meetings and never missed a session. The only thing that ever got in the way of our sessions was sports, which he loved just as much. It didn't matter if it was baseball or basketball he loved it all.

Lamar had been in the group for about eight months. During that time he was able to open up and talk with his housemates. He was learning how to socialize without fear of being hurt or abused.

When he started coming to individual sessions, we got into the habit of making tea and talking, sometimes going over our allotted time. I would even bring in treats once in a while; he particularly loved my cornbread. He said it was like going to his grandmother's house. He felt safe in the art room with me and that was half the battle with Lamar.

Basically, Lamar was a happy kid when he wasn't thinking about his mother. He wasn't looking for charity, and he didn't think the world owed him anything. He was very smart; he told me that his mother had been a nurse; she had a college degree, and loved to read. Lamar would read all kinds of books, and I knew he got his love of reading from her. I would bring him paperback books, and he would take them back to his room. This became his safe haven; he could curl up at night and read in the safety of his own bed.

A lot of the boys here at the agency came from similar backgrounds of trauma and abuse and had severely hampered learning. Lamar had (ADD), Attention Deficit Disorder, which caused him difficulty focusing in a classroom. But his IQ was high, and he had the ability to learn if he could control his impulses. One of my goals for Lamar was to get him to a place where he could relax without fear of being harmed.

When he first came to private sessions, I knew Lamar had no patience for drawing the way Shane did. But he was a great storyteller. So I devised a method of using my reference books to allow him to trace images with tracing paper so he could put them together as illustrations.

One of the stories was about a young knight who befriended a lone wolf. While the knight was out hunting, he came across the wolf who wanted the meat the knight had just captured. The knight shared his kill with the wolf and they became friends.

To me the wolf was Lamar; he was alone, wild and in need of a trusted friend. And he needed to be tamed in order to develop a relationship.

The story continued for many weeks where the two of them went on different adventures together. One such adventure was when they had to combine their skills to combat a two-headed dragon. This, I feel represented his greatest fear.

The two-faced dragon was in his real life drama a monster of untold proportions, unpredictable, dangerous, and needed to be dealt with. The two heads seemed to represent the confusion that his biological mother presented to him. The normal bright woman who loved him and cared for him, and the monster that turned on him, beat him, and abused him.

After about two months the story came to a conclusion. He made a shield for the knight to use to go in to battle with. On the front of the shield was a coat of arms of a wolf with wings. He said the knight and the wolf both represented loyalty, friendship, and protection, three things that Lamar needed to go out into the world with.

But Lamar still had tremendous guilt. He carried the burden of having caused the deterioration of his family and that he was the stressor that caused his mother to do bad things.

As time went on, I discovered that Lamar was the youngest of ten or twelve brothers and sisters. He wasn't sure because he didn't know all of them. His mother hadn't raised any of them and they were all either adopted or in foster care. So how was it that he became the one to bear the burden of a failed family unit?

Lamar said he was the second youngest. When each baby was born if he tested positive for crack cocaine he was immediately placed into foster care, so Lamar and his baby brother were the only two left. His mother held on to Lamar tightly and she didn't want to let him go. She told him that he was different, he was special.

I reminded him that he wasn't a knight in shining armor who was going to save the day. He was just a young boy, and he needed to know that his mother was the one who had to step up and take responsibility for him, not the other way around.

His mother continually told him that it was his fault that he was in placement because of his behavior. He was told that it was up to him to turn it around and learn how to behave before he could go back home. However, Lamar's behavior was a direct response to her erratic behavior.

I drew a picture of a mother with all of these children. I said, "There is a substantial family here. If your mother wants to have a family, they are here, all of them. She had the opportunity to connect with her children." This illustrated to Lamar that he was one of a large group of children who were born into her care. If she hadn't been able to take care of any of them what made him think that she would be able to take care of him?

Now, since Lamar was one of the youngest, she wanted to hang on to him as if it was her last chance to make it right. But the fact still remained she would have to give up the drugs and go straight. He then confided in me and told me this remarkable story.

Evidently, his mother had been dealing with a drug problem for years. Lamar would know what kind of a day he was in for when he got up in the morning. If she was humming and cooking bacon in the kitchen when he woke up, he knew things were okay, but if he woke up and the house was cold and dark and there was a funny bad burning smell in the house, he knew he would have to be on the alert. He didn't know what the smell was but knew it was dangerous, and so he decided to look into it.

As a result of this experience he decided to go to the library. He was only about ten at the time, but nevertheless walked several blocks to find it by himself. He went in and asked to see reference books that would tell him about illegal drugs. As he was reading, when he got to the part about crack, how it was made, how it was smoked and what it smelled like, he knew he had found the culprit. The next thing he wanted to do was figure out a way to make her stop getting it.

He began to follow her as she left the house, and he discovered that she met a man on the street that would sell her little vials of the stuff. And so he decided to try and keep her from leaving the house. He was taking a huge risk, but he thought it was the only way to stop her.

So he took all of her shoes and gave them to the lady who lived downstairs from them in an effort to stop her from leaving. When she discovered what he was up to she went after him. She attacked him with a kitchen knife, threatening to kill him (hence his fear of knives). He ran down the stairs to the neighbor's house, and she called the police. That is how the whole thing unraveled. After that, Child Protective Services was called in and Lamar was put into placement.

I reminded Lamar that he was courageous and desperately wanted to do the right thing. He was not responsible for the choices his mother made. But he was left with the guilt, and took on the thinking that he got his mother into trouble and caused the family to break up.

Given the fact that Lamar was so smart, I needed to appeal to his intellect, but this would take time. Luckily, we were in a residential treatment center which gave us the time to sort out the deeply imbedded issues that needed to be addressed. My belief was that if it took ten years to create, it could take ten years to unravel.

Unlike a psychiatric hospital where most of the treatment was short-term (usually three months at the most) here in this residential setting, I had the luxury of going the distance with Lamar. Their motto in psychiatric hospitals was: "Identify, stabilize, medicate, and discharge." My motto was, "Identify, stabilize, heal, and discharge."

Setting Up the Research

$\mathcal{T}$HE BEAUTIFUL THING ABOUT my research, I felt, was that using guided imagery cut to the quick of deeply imbedded phobias and fears. This was possible by dismantling the client's rigid defense mechanisms. When a child is traumatized, the traumatic effects are magnified tenfold as compared to an adult. Adults can rationalize, get help, look for support, change their situation, or physically fight back. Children have none of these options and therefore tend to be victims, especially when they are very young (Herman, 1992).

In order to survive, a child has to develop an iron clad defense mechanism. It keeps them alive and, in some cases, pushes them into adulthood. Adolescents in particular are very good in protecting their defenses. Most of the time, teens will become oppositionally defiant because they don't want their defense system tampered with in any way (Blos, 1962, p. 143).

A really well-defined defense system can create a sense of safety for most children and sustain them throughout their life; unfortunately, these systems are, most often, maladaptive and disruptive to their ability to help them function as adults (Herman, 1992). That is why it takes so long to develop a trusting relationship with a severely traumatized adolescent. In some cases it has taken me from six months to a year to get a client to open up and talk to me, or even look me in the eye, without their defenses getting in the way.

The guided imagery cuts through all of that, allowing the psyche to relinquish its stronghold on the subconscious. In other words, when the client relaxes, the walls come tumbling down.

What I have found to be consistently true is that most traumatized kids have the ability to visualize very well. It is almost like an innate trait they can tap into at anytime, one that they have developed because of the way they have dissociated in the past, as a defense against trauma. As I have previously explained, the technique of dissociating buys you time. You can escape the trauma and come back when the coast is clear.

Where does the mind wander off to when a person dissociates? I would imagine that it can be as vast and varied as the people that dissociate themselves. Everyone is unique in this regard, and not everyone dissociates but those who do have had to develop this as a way of coping to events that were too overwhelming at the time.

When I was young, one of the coping mechanisms I used was to focus on the things around me, noticing subtly in light and reflection. I suppose that is why I became an artist; my mind would wander off into a space and time that was unlimited because I could see things that most people just didn't notice. For me these things became focal points, like the way the shadow is reflected beneath an object or how the light creates subtle modulations of color as it envelopes an object.

When some people dissociate, they go into a kind of fantasy realm or dream state. This is more in the realm of the imagination, where creativity and visualization reside in the right brain, which becomes activated when the left brain turns off. This phenomenon happens when events that you can't process occur.

The left brain, the logical part, can't compute information that is outside of normal or logical. When the World Trade Center was collapsing, for example, people who witnessed it said it was beyond description; they couldn't find the words to express what they were seeing or feeling. It wasn't until weeks later when they had time to absorb the information that they could then begin to explain in words what the experience was like.

In the same way, when a child is experiencing a traumatic event, such as sexual abuse at a young age, they can't explain it to you in words; they can only express it in images from the right brain. When children dissociate, the mind goes into an altered state, similar to a dream state except instead of being relaxed, the body is hyper aroused (Herman, 1992).

The body records everything but the mind/psyche takes a hiatus. This helps the child escape the traumatic experience, and when the perpetrator is gone, or the situation returns to safety, then the psyche can return. This is the survival mechanism that our species depends on for its continued existence. However, the body remembers the experience and will react when triggered, like when I would get yelled at I would shut down or when someone came at Lamar with a sharp object he would react violently. Without thinking, the body just reacts to the external stimuli because it was programmed to do so in order to survive (Woolger, 1988).

I have had enough trauma in my life to know firsthand what the children I worked with were going through. The trick was to find out what their coping mechanisms were and replace the maladaptive traits with productive coping skills that would serve them better as they reached adulthood.

When I was a child, I retreated into my own world, hiding from danger, afraid to come out. I created an imaginary world full of art and color, a world that I could control, in which I could plan the outcome I desired. As I got older I realized that I had to communicate to the outside world and this is where I ran into trouble. My coping skill didn't translate well into the adult world. I had trouble breaking out of my-self imposed isolation.

When I was in my mid-twenties I received a mailing at my house from the open center in NY City. In the pamphlet was a description of a workshop entitled, "Women's Empowerment". I thought, "This is it; this is exactly what I need," so I signed up.

I was working in New York city at the time as a textile designer and enjoyed my work but still felt isolated, and I wanted to get out there in a bigger way, and I thought this would be perfect.

The presenter was a psychologist named Nancy Napier. She was an expert in the field of psychology and a captivating speaker. In the first half hour of her presentation, she talked about dysfunctional families, and I thought, "Oh! I must be in the wrong workshop; there is nothing wrong with my family." My family was a typical Italian family, loud, emotional but normal, right? I had never heard of anyone coming from a dysfunctional family. I thought that meant you had a parent in jail or some sort of evening-news mass-murder kind of family.

When you are living in a family with domestic violence you think it's normal, that every family is just like yours. No one ever talked about it; no one in my family was allowed to. My trouble focusing in class and dissociating was never picked up as a problem in school. I was considered inattentive, but I wasn't a behavior problem. When my mother went to the hospital after suffering a nervous breakdown she was told she was unable to cope with the rigors of modern day life and family.

My dad was able to conceal and control how my family looked from the outside. Like many abusers they are adept at controlling their prey physically and mentally. So often times it goes undetected. As a child growing up in a home like that you become so accustomed to the dysfunction that you think it is normal. In order for a person to see what their situation is really like they have to step away from it and look at it from the outside.

That was what Nancy Napier did for me. She gave me the platform to stand on so I could see what really happened. Ms. Napier engaged us in a very simple exercise, in what she called guided imagery. This was the first time I ever heard the term.

She demonstrated to me how to relax as I listened to her take me on a journey to meet my child self. I went for a walk through the woods until I came to a clearing, on the other side of the clearing was a young child. As the child came closer into view, it became evident that this child was me when I was younger. Now, since I had mastered the technique of dissociation and I was a visual artist, I had no trouble in visualizing this kind of guided imagery.

What happened to me during this exercise changed my life. The little girl that I met shocked me beyond belief. This girl of around seven years of age was so frightened; I had to coax her out to come and talk to me. When I came face to face with her, she was covered in scars from head to toe. I broke down and cried when I saw her. No wonder she had a hard time coming out into the world; she didn't want anyone to see her. The shame, fear, disgrace, and feelings of unworthiness were all displayed in an ugliness that had scared her for life.

This was the first time I confronted what my life experience had done to me. This was the beginning of a life long journey for me. All I wanted to do was to take that little girl in my arms and tell her everything was going to be okay. That journey had roused in me the awareness to put together the fractured pieces of my broken psyche. Using guided imagery, regression, drawing and dream interpretation helped integrate the frozen bits of information I needed in order to heal. In time I learned how to use these tools. If it could work for me, I knew it could work for others.

For my thesis research, I had written four guided imagery scripts to aid in retrieving bits of lost information. One was to find your own personal symbol designed to inspire your inner growth. The second script was written to guide you to meet your power animal. This idea is taken from ancient cultures as a way to find out what innate traits you have to use for survival. Knowledge of this kind enlightens you and helps you to move forward. Shamans believe that everyone has a power animal. Native Americans teach that animal spirits watch over you, acting like guardian angels. Each power animal that you have increases your power so that illnesses or negative energy cannot enter your body. The spirit also lends you the wisdom of its kind. For example, a hawk spirit will give you hawk wisdom, and give you some attributes of hawk.

"Hawk medicine teaches you to be observant, to look at your surroundings. Observe the obvious in everything that you do to know that life is sending you signals. You are only as powerful as your capacity to perceive, receive, and use your abilities." (Sam & Carson 1988).

The third script was intended to guide you to an imaginary beach and find the message in a bottle. This particular imagery was designed to create a direct link from the sub-conscious mind to the conscious, awake mind. This script never fails to deliver.

The fourth and last journey or script was designed to direct you to confront your greatest terror, in which you come face-to face with a dragon, a real fire breathing dragon. The dragon represents your greatest fear, and how you deal with the dragon is how you will deal with your biggest problem in life. There are several options: you can run, you can stand and fight, you can find helpers to help you fight, you can hide, or perhaps you can even try and negotiate with the dragon. There are many different scenarios you can employ, depending on what your greatest strength is. Your specific reaction to the situation is unique, and will help enlighten you as to your strengths and/or weaknesses.

While the experimental group in the study was being guided into these scripts by inducing relaxation and guiding them through the journey, the control group was being asked to imagine, "If you found a bottle on the beach and it had a message in it for you, what would it say?" Or "If you had a power animal, what animal do you think you would have?" Then they would be asked to draw it. All of the drawings were interesting and spoke specifically to the individual, but, with the experimental group, their drawings were particularly significant. I feel that the subconscious knows exactly what is needed in order to heal a particular complex. I have never seen or experienced a situation in which the individual couldn't relate to the information that he was given. But you have to develop a relationship with the client so that they can trust you enough to relax and allow the information to come to them.

When doing this research, I didn't really know the boys that well, and they didn't know me either, so it was a stretch to push them that far into the recesses of their psyche, especially when they had never done this sort of thing before. That is why I had to take my time and have a few sessions to just get to know them first then I could present information in a secure, delicate way.

Research is time sensitive and scripted in such a way that the experiment has to be done in a specific and orderly fashion. In real time, what would normally take months to uncover and process could happen in one session using guided imagery. But for the sake of science, I had to continue at a rate of one script per week for four weeks and eight weeks for the entire research project.

In a practical sense, I would normally establish a sound base with a client before I would introduce them to guided imagery, and, even then, it is not suited for everyone.

I recall this one boy who I had worked with for about a year. He had been very guarded, and I was asked to see him because no one could get through to him. He didn't trust anyone, and he was an active gang member who had to be watched carefully. He had been running the streets for years before the authorities finally caught up with him.

I somehow managed to keep him engaged in doing art; the miracle was that he came to see me week after week until I felt that he was ready to be introduced to the "dragon" guided imagery.

He was able to visualize like no one I had ever worked with before or since, and he was able to talk about his experience. His story went like this: he traveled to the mountaintop and found the cave. The dragon came out, and he was furious with him for invading his liar. This boy stood there in front of the dragon and was petrified; he said, "The monster was so big and so fierce; I had no defense". He couldn't move, and the dragon breathed fire on him and killed him in an instant.

I was stunned. Here he was this dreaded gang member, with all his vibrato and street smarts, telling me he had no defense against the dragon. I thought for sure he would be able to fight the dragon. That's when I realized, after all of this time working with him, that he was so afraid of the world; he didn't think he could survive out there on his own. He was afraid that he would die, and that was why he had to have a gang around him.

From that point on, my work with him changed, because I knew that I needed to build up his confidence. So that is what we worked on. He was smart and streetwise, but he needed to believe in his own abilities in order to realize that he didn't need a gang to protect him. He covered up his fears so well that if you had met him, you would have thought he was the most confident and self-assured person. But that was just his armor; after the guided imagery cut through the carefully crafted defense mechanism to the real person, I saw the terrified little boy who was hiding inside.

The research continued. I managed to keep all the boys engaged and on track, working to meet my deadline. The pre-tests and post-tests were completed. All of the drawings were collected, and the analysis was compiled. By the time all this was done, it was the end of March. But after the eight-week intervention was completed I still had to track the behaviors for another month. Tracking was important because I wanted to see if the behaviors had improved and if they were sustained over time. This meant that I had to get an extension on my deadline to complete all of the data. This also meant that I couldn't graduate with my class and had to receive my diploma on the next issue cycle, which would be in August. However, it was a small price to pay for getting the data I needed, and for proving my hypothesis.

I summarized my data into four 4-week intervals for each group. In the control group, the behaviors dropped slightly at the end of the second month of the intervention. At the end of the third month, the behaviors dropped to more than half. But after the intervention was completed and tracked for an additional month, the negative behaviors increased slightly.

For the experimental group, at the end of the second month of intervention, the negative behaviors dropped slightly, and at the end of the third month of intervention, the negative behaviors dropped to only a few minor disturbances. After the intervention was completed and tracked for an additional month only one, not-so-serious behavior was reported; to put it another way, the experimental group's negative behaviors had dropped to a 99% reduction in the post-intervention period. This was particularly gratifying, to think that the intervention had sustained its positive effects over time.

The results for depression were measured using the FEATS (Formal Elements of Art Therapy) measurement scale (Gantt & Tabone, 1998). Depression decreased for both groups, but twice as much for the experimental group in the post-intervention period.

As far as estimating their level of creativity, I chose to track the use of color. In the end, the experimental group had an overall increase of 13 points, as opposed to 6.25 for the control group; that was more than double.

Also tracked was implied energy, and the control group had an increase of 0.75, as compared to 4.50 for the experimental group.

The third measurement was the amount of space used on the paper for both the pre and post-test drawings. The control group had a 0.75 decrease in the amount of space used while the experimental group had a 3.0 increase. Together, these results represent an overall 2.25 gain in the amount of space used for the experimental group. I couldn't have been happier with these results; furthermore, I knew they were completely valid. All of the raters used were independent and had no vested interest in the research or knowledge of what the research was about.

This study seemed to confirm the theories that were selected, and would also pose a strong argument for the theory that I call "Image Translation." This theory states that images that arise through visualizations prompted by guided imagery visually translate information from the unconscious to the conscious. Through the art medium the eyes can decode the language of the dream state to a language the conscious mind can understand.

As much as I loved the results of this research I was very careful when I used visualization and guided imagery. Not all of the boys I worked with would be receptive to this kind of intervention. In some extreme cases hyper vigilant kids who had been severely abused could not relax under any circumstances, and would therefore not close their eyes to allow the process to unfold.

Making Puppets

$\mathcal{I}$ HAD BEEN WORKING WITH Alessandro for about eleven months now, and we had gotten to know each other quite well. He continued to come to art therapy once a week for an individual session and he also came once a week as part of a group.

In the group, we started to make puppets and Alessandro's puppet was comprised of a half-good and half-bad puppet. It seemed as if he was still blaming himself for his bad behavior. I would have to admit, assaulting someone wasn't the way to work out your differences, and stealing wasn't acceptable, and he knew that. His puppet was a representation of two separate parts of himself. As he acted the puppets out it became apparent that he was trying to control the negative aspects of his personality.

I could see that Alessandro was preoccupied with this constant battle within himself. He tried to control these urges within him, but there was no way he could stop the negative impulses. He said this conflict was ever present, controlling and exhausting him. The dialogue in his head was debilitating at times, and the only way he could stop it was to sleep.

In his individual session we made a list of all of the things he had learned to do while he was out in the street trying to survive. Stealing was one of them; it was thrilling for him to outsmart people and get away with something that he knew was wrong. He needed to make decisions instantaneously and be quick on his feet, a skill at which he was very adept. He could turn on a dime, avoid people's attention, and leave without being seen or heard. He was fearless in the face of danger. He was an entrepreneur of sorts; he knew how to trade, buy and sell, and negotiate. He had excellent problem-solving skills and most of all, knew how to protect himself. Now, all he had to do was readapt those skills from illegal and inappropriate actions to ones that were lawful and positive.

What could Alessandro do that would employ all of the knowledge he had acquired, and be exhilarating and rewarding at the same time? He needed to consider an activity that was positive, something that he could be proud of.

Alessandro seemed relieved to see that I was not being judgmental about his past discretion. I was instead rather impressed at how brilliant and cunning he was. Not that I condoned any illegal activity, but I knew it was the only way he knew how to survive at the time. He knew he was smart, but, while he was running the streets, he never had time to think about what he was doing. Now that he was away from all of that and in a safe place, he didn't' have to worry about where his next meal was coming from. He could now take the time to look back and see what a challenging journey it had been and where he had gone wrong.

In making the puppets I discovered the reason Alessandro was so torn between his "bad" self and the "good" self. It was due partly because he had so much unresolved anger toward his mother. He had felt abandoned by her; causing him to resent her, which he stuffed down inside creating a split between love and anger, acceptance and guilt.

I knew I couldn't get his mother to change but what I could do was help Alessandro channel some of that hurt and anger into something else that would be beneficial to him. The anger inside of him was causing him to hurt himself and to shut down emotionally. The best remedy for Alessandro would have been to confront his mother with how he was feeling, but she was unavailable for him to do that. He did however begin to discuss his feelings with the masks. He was able to talk to the witch and he was able to tell her how he felt.

That was a start, but there was a whole lot more that was still left unresolved. That was why the only way he could deal with it was to either sleep or pretend to go to his island and isolate himself from everyone.

There was one thing that Alessandro could do to tap into the reservoir of emotion that was trapped inside. Alessandro could release his rage and get his adrenaline rushing with BMX racing. He was hooked on the adrenaline rush he got when he was out there on his bike.

He got a surge of energy and power when he was racing which was what he seemed to be hard wired to do. It is the same adrenaline rush he got during the fight or flight syndrome, (you will find that people who have had a lot of highly charged activity in their past will sometimes continue pursuing interests that repeat high adrenaline scenarios). He kept trying to suppress these urges but it was leaving him feeling exhausted.

The BMX racing he found thrilling, and exhilarating. He had to think quickly on his feet, problem-solve automatically, and it gave him the adrenaline rush he was missing. The racing had a plus side to it as well; it was legal, and he received accolades from his friends when he won, which was the same feeling he got when he supplied them with stolen goods.

Alessandro was able to sublimate a lot of his negative behaviors and trapped emotions by channeling his energy into BMX racing. He immediately started building a mini race track in the art room, with jumps and turns. It had all the daredevil excitement of a real track. As it turned out, he was able to join a team and compete on the weekends when he went home. It was also something he could do with his dad and grandfather, so it became a real family event. The agency even allowed him to build a somewhat modified version of a track on the campus so Alessandro could practice during the week.

The BMX racing helped Alessandro in releasing pent up frustration by providing him with the feeling of acceptance from his friends and family, and it was something he was proud of. Alessandro was spending more and more time with his family and his behavior was now improving in his residence since he had a way to release his pent up emotions.

There was talk about moving him to a more independent house which would be the last step toward his discharge. But there was one very big looming question still hanging over Alessandro's head. He knew for sure his mother was out of the picture; her rights had been terminated but he still needed to decide where his true allegiance lay. Did he want to live with his father or did he want to go with his grandfather?

His father was in denial about his responsibilities, which left Alessandro feeling vulnerable and afraid that he would never get discharged.

I felt we needed clarification as to whom he felt more allegiance to. It was time for Alessandro to let his true feelings emerge about his hidden longing. In doing so he was directed into another guided imagery called, "Meeting the Dragon"

The script took Alessandro through a relaxation exercise in order for him to calm down enough to allow the images of his hidden feelings to surface. Then he was guided to travel up the mountain, in his imagination, to where the cave was.

He climbed and climbed until he found the cave. What happened next was significant in terms of the symbolism that came to him. This type of imagery falls into what I call, "you-just—can't-make-this-stuff-up"category!

He found the cave and when he looked into the cave, he saw the dragon, and, low and behold, the dragon was asleep. You would think that he would be afraid of the dragon, try and run or hide or something, but no, Alessandro decided to wake him up by throwing a rock at his head and he hit him right in the eye.

Of course, the dragon woke up and was in a really bad mood, as he looked around he found this young boy standing there in front of him. Alessandro stood his ground and did not run. Interestingly enough, the dragon started whimpering and wiping his badly bruised eye.

Now, Alessandro jumped into action, and, instead of running away, he ran toward the dragon and leapt up onto his neck and started cleaning the wound and applied healing salve to it.

At this point, the dragon stopped his whimpering and acted as if he wanted to play with him. Alessandro started to talk to him and told him he was sorry for hitting him in the eye, but he needed to wake him up and get his attention. The dragon seemed to be longing for his company and accepted the boy's apology and asked him to be his friend.

Alessandro jumped on his back, and, together, they flew up into the sky. The dragon asked him, "Where do you want to go?" Alessandro replied, "I want to go home." The drawing he made was of the two of them flying home.

This, to me, was a truly extraordinary story that needed to be processed to find out what the symbolism meant to Alessandro. First, I needed to find out who he needed to wakeup. He said it was his dad; his dad was sleeping and needed to wake up and see him and hear him.

Interestingly, Alessandro hit him in the eye, making a special point of directing the imagery to the eye, which is what he needed to wake up and "SEE" his son. Evidently, his dad was not paying attention to his son and needed to take responsibility for him. His dad may also have been preoccupied with healing his own wounds and thus didn't have time to see or hear his son.

What was important here was the fact that it was up to Alessandro to make his dad notice him. It was imperative for his dad to hear from Alessandro in order to learn about his needs and it was Alessandro's responsibility to tell him. Alessandro wanted to go home and he wanted his dad to take him there.

Alessandro's greatest fear was that his dad wouldn't wake up and see him in order to take responsibility for him. The good news was that in the guided imagery he did get his attention and they were able to go home together.

This gave Alessandro new hope in a repaired relationship with his dad. In the past Alessandro had always gone to the grandfather allowing the dad to shirk his responsibilities. That had to change, and it was up to Alessandro to make his dad aware of his needs.

In the meantime, he was going home on Saturdays giving him the time needed to make his interests known and to have the necessary conversation with him. His father had work to do to get his life straightened out and to make the urgent changes in order to become the responsible parent he needed to be.

It was still uncertain where Alessandro would wind up, but one thing was for sure; his mother was not being considered a discharge resource and his dad needed to step up and take charge.

Getting in Touch with the Source

SHANE CONTINUED TO COME to art therapy sessions, but he was still relying on copying material from superhero books that he got out of the library. He wasn't totally drawing on his own yet in session with me. He also relied on me to lay out the composition for the preliminary sketches. Once the drawing was laid out, Shane would then put in all of the details and shading.

I wanted him to draw more from his imagination, so I made a deal with him. I told him that I'd help him with one drawing if he'd do a second one for me on his own, on a theme of my choice. He agreed, so we proceeded.

One of the first directives I gave him was: 'How do you see yourself in the future?' He drew a picture of a very determined young man walking to an art studio with a portfolio under his arm.

Shane drew a lot on his own outside of the studio, but he was reluctant to draw in front of me. I guess he was still self conscious about his ability, yet he had his own folder that he would take everywhere he went. He even asked me questions about art school, and wanted to know which programs were the best in the area. He also wanted to know what he had to do to get accepted. This was all good news as far as Shane was concerned. He had begun to build up ego strength and was now thinking about his future. He was taking better care of himself too.

By March, I had been working with Shane for about ten months. He was excited about his upcoming birthday so I used that as an access point to gather information about him. I asked him if there was one gift he could have, anything at all, what would it be? He said he would have liked to have never been in foster care.

He then started to draw a picture of people who looked like aliens. He said that these aliens were coming to earth to eat us. It appeared that the aliens were a metaphor for the people he had to live with throughout the years and perhaps even a symbol of how he felt about himself, feeling like an alien that didn't fit in anywhere.

Shane hardly ever missed a session now, and to think that it was just a few months ago that he wanted to quit! I believe that once he got over his fear of failing, he came into his own. Shane had been trying to make sense of his world through his art. He expressed himself better through images than words.

I had to make sure that he stuck to the contract we had made: he could draw one image from a book and one image from his imagination. This way, I could get him to tap into his subconscious and dislodge the buried trauma he had stored there.

One of his first drawings of this sort was a picture of a car. Symbolically, it suggested to me traveling and hopefully moving forward. I proposed he draw a map for the car so that we could get an idea of where he wanted to go. Shane drew a ramp that sent the car hurling through space and straight up into the heavens.

I said, "This is like a spaceship! Where is it going?"

Shane said, "It's going to hell. Well, not really, I want to go to heaven. I could kill myself right now and go there."

I knew Shane had tried to kill himself several times before, so I didn't doubt the sincerity of his statement.

"So you want to go to heaven. Who do you want to see in heaven?"

He said, "I want to talk to my dad. I just want to see him."

"Okay, what do you want to say to him?"

"I just want to say hello."

"What do you think he would say?" I asked.

"He would say 'hi.'"

"What do you think he is doing up there?"

Shane said, "I don't know. He used to like to drink, so I guess he is just hang'en around in bars and stuff."

I continued, "So when you get up there, do you think he will know who you are?"

He said, "Oh yeah, he knows me."

"Really, how do you know?" I inquired.

"He knows me because he is up there watching me all the time."

"All right, who else is up there watching you?"

He had my interest now.

"I have an aunt and my grandparents."

"Great, what do you think they would want for you?"

"I don't know," said Shane.

"I think they would want you to grow up and live your life and be happy. What do you want?"

"I want to go to art school and do well," Shane responded.

"So there you go! If you put your mind to it, you will go to art school and you will do well," I said encouragingly.

Throughout his ten years of therapy, this poor boy had been tormented by living in the shadow of a man he never knew. I began to realize that Shane was trying to identify with a homeless man by emulating him, trying to be like him.

Of course, this wasn't intentional, but Shane looked like a homeless person. He didn't bathe properly, even though our staff desperately tried to get him to do so. He didn't clean his clothes, and, oftentimes, he would wear the same dirty shirt over and over again.

After this session of the car going to heaven, he seemed to open the door to finally talk about his father. It was as if he was asking me to journey with him to this place; uncharted territory in which he seemed afraid to go to alone. This was where he wanted to go, to talk to his dad, but I didn't want to push him there. It had to come from him. All I could do was set the stage for him to explore and be there with him in case it became too stressful for him.

In the next session, I asked him to do a scribble drawing. He drew a large mess of swigged lines all over the paper. I asked him to look at it, to really study it and see if he could see anything in the scribble.

He saw something in it. This was what his subconscious wanted him to see; this was the key we were looking for. He saw a long boney and gnarled fingernail that was pointing toward a balloon that it was going to prick and deflate.

Who was this mystery man who was going to pop his balloon?

I then asked Shane to highlight the images that he saw and bring it to life so that it could emerge from the scribbled lines. He did this, and this new image became our story line. Shane drew a second image of two figures. One was like a ghost standing behind a little boy. In this drawing, the ghost appeared to be holding back the little boy. He seemed to have his arm around him.

I asked Shane if this was the ghost who popped his balloon. He said yes and that he was mad at him for popping the balloon. Yet he wanted to apologize to the ghost for being mad at him. I asked him, "Why do you feel the need to apologize? After all, wasn't he the one who popped your balloon?" I went on to say, "You didn't do anything to him."

"Yeah, right," said Shane.

I knew that Shane was desperately trying to befriend the man who was his father and that he wanted so much to be loved by him. Shane said he wanted to make peace with the ghost, but, every time Shane tried to shake hands with him, his hand became invisible.

It was true that the old man was holding Shane back. Ever since he had died, Shane was frozen in time just like him. In his attempt to be like his dad, he froze on that park bench along with him.

A part of Shane died with his dad when he was five years old. That is why the image of a man popping his balloon is so fitting because it all happened around the time of his fifth birthday. This man, Shane's father, drank himself to death and froze on a park bench. To emulate this man, to feel like a part of his father's life, Shane became just like him an unkempt vagabond, foregoing washing and taking care of himself to live in his father's shadow.

This was quite a huge step for Shane, the biggest one he had taken since I had started working with him, and I felt he was ready for the next leap. In the very next session, I asked Shane to draw me a picture of the old man.

He drew a very poignant picture of a man who looked like an older version of him. I took the drawing and put it up on the wall on the opposite side of the room from where we were standing. I then instructed Shane to tell the old man what was on his mind.

The word father never came up. We were working completely in metaphor. If I interjected or imposed the idea that this was an image of Shane's father, I would have shattered the line of trust we had together. I had to keep it in the imaginary realm where Shane could access him. After all, he was only a ghost . . . but one that had a powerful hold on Shane.

Shane mumbled something under his breath. I had to ask him to repeat what he said.

"What did you say? I can't hear you," I stated.

He said, "I'm still mad at you for popping my balloon."

G. C. De Pietro

I then remembered how just a few weeks ago Shane was so excited about his upcoming birthday. I could just see the little five-year-old boy waiting for his father to come to his party. How disappointed he would be when his father didn't show up.

I then did something un-conventional but very instinctive. I gave Shane a Wiffle ball and asked him to throw it at the picture to see if he could hit the man. I knew that Shane was frozen, just as frozen as that man on the park bench, and he needed to move so that he could unfreeze and come back to life.

Shane just lopped the ball in the direction of the picture. It didn't even reach the wall.

I said, "Shane, you are a big, strong guy; you can do better than that! I've seen you play baseball out there. You can throw a ball." I handed it back to him and said, "Let's see what you can do with it this time. But as you throw it, I want you to tell him how mad you are at him for popping your balloon."

He threw it again, this time a little bit harder than the first, and he said, "You popped my balloon."

But he just sort of said it like "how are you today."

I said, "I thought you were mad at him. Try it again and, this time, mean it."

Shane threw it again and this time he was louder,

"YOU POPPED MY BALLOON."

"Good, now hit him with the ball this time," I said.

Again, he threw it. This time, he hit the man right in the head. I started cheering from the sidelines. "Yeah, you did it! You hit him; you got him. Hit him again!" I handed him the ball.

This time he threw it really hard and yelled,

"YOU POPPED MY BALLOON." Shane threw it with everything he had in him and hit the man right in the face.

"What else do you want to tell him, Shane?" I asked.

"YOU, YOU BROKE MY MOTHER'S HEART. SHE DESPISES YOU." "Good, Shane. Keep going," I said, handing

— 84 —

him the ball, "Throw it again." "**YOU SENT ME INTO FOSTER CARE, YOU HURT ME, AND I HATE YOU**."

"Hit him again, Shane. What else do you want to tell him?"

"**YOU ONLY THOUGHT ABOUT YOURSELF, YOU NEVER THOUGHT ABOUT US**."

Now he was really throwing it with all of his might, and he was screaming out the ten years of hurt that had been buried inside of him. He was sweating and crying and yelling. His face was beet red and he just kept hitting him and yelling, "**YOU RUINED MY LIFE, MY MOTHER'S LIFE**."

Finally, the picture fell to the floor and Shane ran over to it, jumping and stomping on it yelling. "**I HATE YOU, I HATE YOU, I HATE YOU, I HATE YOU**."

Finally, he stopped. He was balling his eyes out, crying as he fell to the floor. I went over to him and picked him up and hugged him.

I said, "Good job, Shane. You really told him; you got the last word. Come on, sit down and relax. You need to rest."

I got him to come over to the table and sit. He was shaking. He sat down and wrote a list of all of the things he said and drew one last picture.

Shane really let it all out, and he was exhausted. He needed to go home and rest. He was spent, but, now, for the first time, he could go home and be his own person. He didn't have to live in the shadow of the ghost any longer.

The Flood

$\mathcal{I}$ WAS STILL WORKING IN the basement of one of the residences; this was not the best situation but was better than working out of my car. The room was small with little light because the windows were small and high up, but it was cozy and quiet down there, away from the noise of disciplining by the line staff up on the main floor.

What I needed was wall space that I could display the boys' work on and more storage space for the art supplies. Because I was functioning as an independent worker within an already established structure there wasn't much of a budget allocated for what I was doing. I wasn't officially affiliated with any arm of the agency, not the Recreation Department, or the Psychology Department. I wasn't a social worker, and I wasn't part of the line staff who worked in the houses; I was totally on my own.

Therefore, as a free agent I was limited in my estimates for budgeting. I was working with a meager $50.00 a year per child for art supplies. Little by little, I began to build up the art supply list. Over time, I collected found objects, cardboard boxes, legos, wood scraps, and all kinds of sewing materials. I was continuously building up a supply of valuable materials. What I didn't know was that all of my efforts were about to be compromised.

It was spring, and no one had warned me that, during the rainy season, the houses were prone to flooding. When I got to work one rainy April morning, routinely running into the residence from my car, carrying an arm full of supplies that I thought I would need for that day. Suddenly, I stopped short at the bottom of the stairs. Something looked strange, and I couldn't quite put my finger on it.

I looked down into the dark room, and it seemed as if everything was floating. I took the last step and my foot went squish. The carpet was soaked and there was about a foot of water in the art room. I didn't know what to do. I couldn't believe my eyes.

The smell was sour and strange, like decayed plaster and rotten mold. I wanted to open the windows, but it was still pouring outside. The walls of the studio were bubbling and buckling from all of the moisture. Every folder that held the boys' artwork was on the floor at the bottom of the closet which had soaked up all the water around it. There was black mold growing on the walls, the room was completely ruined, along with all the artwork.

It was Monday, so, all weekend the water had been pouring into the basement. All I could do was call maintenance. I was having a hard time breathing down there, but stayed because I needed to try and save as much of the artwork as I could. I was afraid to use the phone, so I went upstairs to use the main house phone. Evidently, maintenance didn't think I was a priority, and I had to wait a long time for them to get there. In the mean time, I was trying to salvage whatever I could and place it up high out of the water.

Eventually, maintenance came and informed me that somehow the sump pump had stopped working. It must have been the power failure over the weekend; the pump never went back on, so the water just built up. No one had thought to check the basement after three days of rain, and, now, it seemed as if everything was ruined. Even the cabinets and furniture were buckling. I cancelled all of my sessions for the day, as I needed time to sort everything out.

After several hours of trying to move things out, my allergies started acting up, and I started to feel sick. The black mold was starting to get to me. Since all maintenance could do was assess the situation, they left without doing much of anything. The maintenance guy Sam said they needed to get a wet vac. and get the sump pump working, which needed outside assistance. Nothing much was going to be accomplished that day.

By the time I went home, I was exhausted and I felt as if no one was interested in what happened to the art room or the work the boys had done. No one ever offered to help me move things to higher ground. I was starting to feel like I was on a raft alone in the middle of the ocean.

The following morning the sunshine helped me cope. I was never so happy to see it. I brought a huge tarp from home and set it up in the yard. Little by little, I brought everything outside. The folders all had multiple pieces of paper in them that had stuck together. The markers had run, and the drawings started too looked like watercolor paintings.

I had to separate each piece of paper and lay them out in the sun with paperweights on them to hold them down so they could dry out. The big problem was that it was also a very windy day, and anything not weighted down would just blow away. I spent a lot of time that day running through the field gathering pieces of paper.

The artwork was precious to me. It documented the boys' progress and accomplishments over months of hard work. Their innermost thoughts and feelings were etched into those papers. The boys had experienced so much loss in their lives, I couldn't bear to see their efforts crumble into bits of saturated rubble.

When the boys got out of school, some of them came over to help me, mostly Shane and Lamar. But they all had schedules to keep, I couldn't really expect them to take the time to help me so, the cleanup was left up to me.

After the paper dried out, I didn't know what to do with them or where to keep them. The yard was starting to look like a rummage sale, attracting a lot of attention. Most staff members would walk by just shaking their heads saying, "What a shame that all of this stuff got ruined," but no helpers came forward.

All of the cardboard and poster board had to be thrown out. All the paper was useless, fabric had to be washed and dried, most of the paints and brushes were okay, but everything needed to be cleaned and dried. This was going to be a long week, and I had no idea when the art room would be ready to work in again. The mold was still growing on the walls, and I just couldn't breathe down there.

I told my supervisor that even if they fixed the sump pump, I didn't think I could go back and work down there. So I guessed it was back to working out of my car once again.

This was such a letdown. I gathered what materials I could and put them in my car. I felt like a traveling salesman with everything I owned in the back seat.

Maintenance finally got there with fans and a wet vac. to soak up the water, but the carpet smelled so bad they couldn't salvage it. I worked out of my car for the next few weeks while the heaters and the fans dried out the basement. I eventually returned, but it wouldn't be long before I would be moving out of there altogether.

During my breaks, I started looking around for another studio space and asked everyone I knew if they could spare some room. I came to find out that space was a high commodity on campus that everyone seemed to want more of.

I noticed a little house; it was like a little bungalow that seemed to be abandoned. I never saw anyone coming or going in or out of it, so I started poking about, looking in the windows, and inquiring about it. It looked like it was full of boxes and junk.

By this time I knew all of the guys in the maintenance department, so I asked them about it. They told me that it was once used for the boys' choir as a music room. I was surprised I didn't know they ever had such a thing.

Sam, the head of maintenance, told me there was a man who worked at the school as a music director for fifty years.

He even had a steel drum band, but after he died he was never replaced, and his music room became a catch-all for old computers, desks, broken chairs, and boxes.

I asked him if he thought I could use the room as an art room. He said he didn't know, but that this particular house was part of the recreational arm of the facility. Sam said he would talk to the powers that be to see if I could use it. At this point, it seemed like only a miracle could solve my problem.

Evidently, the Recreation Department was about to go through a huge transition. I had never formally met the director of that department so I made an appointment to meet with him. He was a young guy who seemed to be interested in making the Rec. Department a substantial part of the boys' curriculum. To be honest, the facility he was in seemed pretty rundown. He had all to do to keep what he had up and running, never mind having time to think about another building, which was clear on the other side of the campus. He said he couldn't really use that house at the moment, but that didn't mean he might not need it in the future. It looked as if it was available, which at the time was very good news to me. He wasn't promising I could use it indefinitely; he just said I could use it temporarily; lucky for me he was preoccupied with other things at the moment.

The Rec. director said that in exchange for my use of the vacant house, I would run some art programs over the summer. So that was the deal we made. But he was adamant about my not doing art therapy with the kids only art.

I never thought he would be interested in art therapy, so I didn't give it a second thought. This decision would come to haunt me later. I said, "Okay, that won't be a problem," and we shook hands on it.

Sam, from maintenance, had keys for everything, so, one day, he took me over to take a look inside the old house. It was amazing. It was a Tudor-style house built in the twenties with a fifteen-foot ceiling and windows all around. It was about three hundred and sixty square feet inside with a chalkboard on one wall and windows on the other three. It was, however, filled to the brim with all kinds of junk. I started going in on Saturdays to clean it out while I kept after Sam to help.

I met him there early one Saturday morning and helped him load three truckloads full of junk out of the space. It looked so big without all of that stuff piled up in there. I found the risers that the old choir stood on, a box of sheet music, steel drums, old photos, and boxes of stuff. It was like a time warp everything left there was just petrified in time.

The photos were really neat. I kept some of them because they were historic. Also, the CEO of the agency was somewhat of a history buff on this place, he was collecting photos, so I thought he might like them. I decided to save them for him and put them in a safe place to deal with another day.

I received permission for the boys to help me clean out the space as sort of an on-site work project. The boys were great, and the experience really helped them bond together by working for a common cause. I told them it would eventually be a place where they could come and be creative. This was something they could all get excited about. They were fantastic! They washed windows and swept up the floor, cleaned the windowsills and so on. The place hadn't been touched in about twenty years, so you could imagine the dirt and grime that had built up.

Lamar was the funniest; he said, "Ms. G, this place is worse than the projects."

I said, "But just you wait and see what we turn this into!"

He kept shaking his head saying, "no way, it's just too messed up."

I had renovated quite a few old houses with my husband over the years. It was sort of a side job for us where we would buy properties, fix them up, and then sell them, so I was used to this kind of work, and I knew what to do.

I went every Saturday for weeks. I bought putty for the windows where the old glass had lost its glazing. There were a few holes in the floor in which I had asked maintenance to come and fix, but they never found the time to help me out. I found some missing floor tiles that I put back in place, but the floor always remained somewhat needy.

I begged and borrowed for cabinets, tables, and chairs. I even bought some utility tables for the boys to use to do their artwork on. I was tired of working out of my car, and wanted to remodel this house as fast as I could so I could start working in it. I started painting the walls; I couldn't wait for maintenance to get around to it. I painted the walls as far up as I could reach with a small ladder that maintenance gave me. But there were some serious leaks in the ceiling and around the windows that wouldn't be easy to paint over. The hallway was in particularly bad shape, with terrible water stains around the windows. I did the best I could with soap and water and paint, but I could only do so much. I found this stain resistant paint at the hardware store that did a pretty good job at covering up the mess, but the roof needed looking after, and I knew that was a big job because it was really old and would probably need to be replaced. So I just did what I could.

It was amazing what a new coat of paint could do. Once the walls were painted, the place really started to look a lot better. But I could only reach up so far and the ceiling in the center of the room had to be at least fifteen feet high. I was not going to get hurt trying to get to it, so I asked maintenance again if they could help me with the painting, but no one ever came.

The plumbing was also a mess. The only sink was at the end of the hall, and it was pretty stopped up I found it hard to wash up after painting. I was starting to get frustrated. Sam seemed like a nice guy, but he never followed through with anything. But at least the space was clean and bright enough to start working in, so I could finally stop working out of my car.

The room was about eighteen feet by twenty feet, with lots of sunlight coming in the windows on all three sides and the fourth had a chalkboard. It was pretty awesome. If I didn't look up and see the old, unpainted, dirty ceiling it was okay. I was basically ready to pretend that it wasn't there. Maintenance had replaced the bulbs in the fluorescent lights that hung down about ten feet, so when the lights were on, you didn't notice the ceiling that much.

I had managed to create my dream studio for the boys. It was a lot of hard work, but we all enjoyed it so much. I couldn't wait to show it off. Believe it or not, I had been working there for over a year already and moving into the space was sort of a celebration of that achievement.

I had gotten enough storage cabinets and furniture to allow the boys to come over for sessions. I had a desk and a computer set up with a phone, so I was ready to get to work. The desk was situated on the opposite side of the entrance door so I could see whoever might enter. After all, I was there alone most of the time, and I needed to be careful.

In the other corner were bookshelves for reference materials and across from that were some leather arm chairs with a round table that was designated for relaxing, having tea, and talking. It made it feel homey. I used to love to sit there in the wintertime and watch the snow come down. But most of all, I liked the light. I had been in the basement for so long that sunlight was a real treat.

I was able to purchase some table easels for painting, which I knew Shane would enjoy. Once everything was set up it started to feel like a real art studio.

Since I had been working so hard on the space I was looking forward to my vacation in August. I asked maintenance one more time about painting the ceiling. I gave them the dates I would be gone so they could get in and finish the ceiling. I would be gone for three weeks; I thought that would be enough time to get the job done. I really needed to take a break. The studio was a lot of hard physical work which was carried out while I maintained a full roster of therapy sessions. It was a daunting task, but necessary, I felt good about it because I was creating a space that was like a professional art studio that the boys could come to and feel special in. Yeah, I felt tired but it was a good tired; the kind of worn-out you get when you've worked really hard and accomplished something great.

"The Studio" by De Pietro

But surprise, surprise! When I got back from vacation, nothing had been done. The ceiling still wasn't painted, I was so disappointed.

Starting a New Year

$\mathcal{I}$ WAS OPTIMISTIC ABOUT THE future and felt I had come a long way since I started volunteering a little over a year ago. Now that I had finished my thesis and graduated, I could finally get my license from the state of New York.

Once I got my license, my plan was to supervise interns so that I could have them help me run more groups. There were several units on campus. My plan was to have one intern for each unit, who would provide art therapy for the residents in that unit. I would then supervise the interns.

It was customary that interns would work for school credit, so having art therapy available to the entire campus wouldn't add any cost to the agency, and all the children would have an opportunity to get the therapy they needed. As it was now, not all of the kids on the campus received therapy. There were a limited amount of residents that each psychologist and psychiatrist could see during any given week.

In theory, the agency wanted each child to receive therapy, but if they weren't a behavior problem, often times they didn't' get treatment. The ones they did see were often being monitored for medications and at best were only seen for one hour a week, but some of these kids needed much more than that. After all, wasn't the whole idea of residential care to get the children back on their feet, emotionally, and mentally, so they could become productive, independent citizens in society?

I had always thought that part of the plan for putting a child into residential treatment was to help them get the counseling they needed. I knew that not all of the residents in the house I was working in saw a psychologist on a regular basis.

Also not all the boys responded well to traditional therapy, I thought that art therapy would be the best way to reach the kids that couldn't verbalize their problems with a psychologist. Especially, since the limited time I was there, I saw positive results with the more resistant boys who weren't helped by the traditional methods.

I made an appointment to see the CEO of the agency to talk to him about my ideas. I knew he was very interested in the history of the agency and had an archive of documents and photographs dating back to its earliest days. I thought he might want to see the photos I had uncovered in the renovation of the studio and I wanted to thank him for the opportunity to create an art therapy office on the campus.

He was truly appreciative for my contribution of photographs I had uncovered. And he seemed truly interested in my proposal; especially since I didn't think it would cost the agency much, if anything to implement my ideas. I was only interested in being paid for the extra hours it would take for me to supervise the interns. He said he would think about it.

My supervisor was also encouraging me to move up. She said, now that I had my master's degree and my credentials, I should be paid a professional salary and not be paid as an intern any longer. I followed her lead and spoke to the Human Resources Department (HR) about getting a raise as a professional therapist instead of an intern in training.

What happened next was truly startling. HR got back to me and said that they had never asked me to go on and get credentialed, that it wasn't important to them whether I had added letters to my name; they didn't think it was necessary for the job I was doing. But I had explained to them that I couldn't work in the state without having a license, and, in order for me to even be able to take the (LCAT) Licensed Creative Art Therapy exam, I had to have a master's degree.

That didn't seem to matter to them. They didn't feel obligated to give me more money, and didn't want me to supervise any additional interns. And to make matters worse, they didn't want to put any more money into the space I was using. The ceiling never got painted, the floor remained incomplete and I had to continue on working with no incentive to expand the art therapy department.

Art therapy didn't seem to be a priority, for whatever reason, even if it wasn't going to cost them more money for me to have interns on the campus. They didn't want to pay me to supervise them. This didn't make any sense to me. Everyone I worked with, the psychologists, and staff members, were all very happy with the work I was doing. I couldn't figure out why the administration wouldn't be interested in giving these kids the extra support they needed. Unless they were not convinced that art therapy was really effective, maybe they didn't think they needed it on their campus.

Either way I was still going to continue seeing the boys I was already seeing, but I thought I should be paid for the extra day per week it would take me to supervise the interns. I felt strongly about that. Why shouldn't I be paid a professional wage?

Now, I was feeling as if no one really cared about the work I was doing. I wasn't bringing in any recognition to the campus, and it wasn't generating any income for them. The bottom line was that they hadn't advertised for an art therapist. I just showed up, so, now, I should just be quiet and be thankful that I had a job.

Oddly enough, I became the envy of the campus because my space was one of the nicest. If only they knew what I had gone through to get it to look the way that it did. People were starting to talk about the work I was doing with the kids too. Residents were being referred to me all the time.

I was seeing children from outside the original twelve. Now, I was seeing kids from the whole unit. I was seeing about twenty-five kids a week, and, with my meetings and paper work on top of that, I was there full-time and I needed every minute of it.

One of the houses I began to work with was right across the street from the studio, which made it convenient for me to see them. They became an interesting group. It started out as the residence for special education. This particular group consisted of boys who were a year or two behind their grade level. Most of these boys were fourteen and fifteen years of age, but were at a second and third grade reading level.

The administration thought the main focus would be to help them with their studies and get them back up to grade level, but it became abundantly clear within a very short time that these boys had a lot of psychiatric problems as well.

I started seeing quite a few of the boys from that house. What was also a startling reality was that these boys needed a lot more hands-on disciplining than what had originally been planned for. The administration quickly realized that they were understaffed and ill-equipped to handle the amount of physical outbursts that happened on a daily basis.

I started working with these boys, uncovering the traumas that led to their psychological breakdowns. It was startling. One boy had been molested as a child and witnessed his father's murder. He could not verbalize the details of the events that led to his dysfunction, but it all came out in the artwork that he made.

Another boy had been traumatized by the gangs in his neighborhood and had been selling drugs to other kids since he was about eleven years old. His fear of going to school prevented him from returning on a regular basis. It wasn't because he didn't want to go to school, he loved school, but he was afraid of the gangs. He was one of the smartest kids in the group and one of the few who thrived under our protection and supervision.

Another boy was emotionally disturbed from having been adopted and then rejected by his adopted parents and sent back to the foster care system. Evidently,there was little information about his birth mother. I felt that there was some early preverbal trauma that was difficult for him to access. Some of the images that came out in his drawings had to do with a drowning in a river, but it was all very vague.

Each one of these boys had serious problems that an average public school was ill-equipped to handle. Yet, one thing was for certain: as their traumatic problems were dealt with, their behavior and even their IQ's seemed to improve.

In general, the type of children that were coming to the Residential Treatment Center (RTC) these days seemed to have more serious problems than the common neglect case that was the norm. Part of this was because of the increase in unemployment in the state and the increase in inflation that caused more and more families to fall below the poverty line.

When I was a kid growing up in the '60s, the average cost of a home was $12,700.00, the average income was $5,315 a year, and the price of gasoline was twenty-five cents a gallon. In 2013, the average cost of a home is $200,000, the average income is $35,000.00 dollars a year, and the price of gasoline is approximately $3.60 per gallon. The difference between the haves and the have-nots was getting wider. In 1960, there was an 11% unemployment rate, and in 2013 the unemployment rate is about 8.5 % not taking into account those who ran out of their unemployment benefits, and those who were underemployed (statistics on wikapedia.org).

The real difference between then and now is that there are more people living in the United States today than in 1960. We have jumped from 179 million inhabitants to 308 million. Approximately 190,000 people were living in poverty in the 60s, compared to the 46.2 million people living in poverty today. And that number is on the rise (www.census.gov.).

Forty six million people would have been a quarter of the entire population of 1960 living in poverty, but, in today's figures it is only about fifteen percent. But that is a huge amount of people, and I don't think we have the resources to handle it, especially when the state is broke and reluctant to send kids into treatment (www.census.gov.).

Most residential treatment centers are far below capacity. The amount of kids estimated to become homeless this year is 1.5 million. Yet homes and shelters are closing all across the nation. Mental hospitals are closing and the unemployment rate continues to rise (Children's Bureau, U. S. Depart. of Health & Human Services).

The state isn't sending children into residential treatment because it costs an average of $60,000 per child per year for residential resources. Instead, the state has been trying to send the resources to the families. This is called the MST program, which stands for Multi-Systemic Therapy. They send the tutors, therapists, and social workers to the families and try to keep the children in their own homes. In theory, this is a great idea, but, in reality, a lot of these kids would be better off away from their families.

It seems to be a vicious cycle. The higher the unemployment, the higher the number of kids at risk and the more pressure there is on law enforcement and other resources to keep the status quo. The higher the unemployment, the higher the foreclosure and the less taxable retable's there are, as in property tax which pays for the treatment centers. As the social network becomes unstable, we all become more mentally fragile.

We know what happens when kids run wild in the streets in gangs that are out of control. There are so many neighborhoods in the city that the cops don't even want to go in to. So what is the answer? Education is critical in breaking the cycle. We must be dedicated to keeping our kids in school, and the ones that can't stay in school need to be helped in other ways in order to become successful, independent, and socially responsible adults.

Most of the kids in the unit I was working with had learning disabilities. But because of their abhorrent discipline problems, they weren't accepted into regular schools. In whatever way we can, as a society, we need to pull together on this. They aren't criminals, but if left outside of the system, they would most likely become criminals, without an education how will they become employed, how will they make a living? If one falls, we all fall. The majority of lawmakers don't see the big picture. A child that doesn't get help early on will cost the system tenfold later. What one mother fails to do, it takes an entire village to pull together to do.

We live in one of the most affluent countries in the world. We need to step up to this challenge. Children are not born evil or bad, but when terrible things happen to them, they get traumatized, they become out of control, angry, and sometimes they seem unreachable. But, underneath it all they are just kids. Is it too much to ask to give them the things they need? I don't think so.

Elijah, Hold On To Your Heart

I WAS INTRODUCED TO A new arrival at the home. I was saying goodbye to Alessandro therefore had a spot open to take on a new client. This new kid was about 15 years old, tall and thin, wore glasses, and seemed to be extremely suspect. He tended to stay to himself, and was hovering in the corner of the house stairwell when I first saw him. He appeared to me to be experiencing, a high level of post traumatic stress. When I went to talk to him for the first time he was cowering in the corner of the landing. He was refusing to come down and get into program. He blocked the other boys who were trying to get past him on the stairs, causing an even more stressful situation.

The more staff tried to reason with him by coaxing him to come down from the stairs the more agitated he became. He seemed to be like a stray that was cornered and frightened, he became so distressed that he started howling like a dog.

I was stunned to see such a display as this; he seemed dissociated, experiencing a complete break with reality. Staff informed me that he spent a lot of time meowing and barking like an animal. He refused to get into program so staff just left him alone.

I approached him slowly as if I was trying to gain the trust of a wild animal. I spoke in low soft tones and didn't get to close. I didn't want to startle him. I introduced myself to him; I told him what I did, and invited him to come to the art room. I told him he would be safe there and that none of the other kids would be there. I told him that it would be his private time, and he could choose to do artwork or just sit if he wanted to. It was up to him.

I asked him if he understood what I had just told him. He nodded in reply. I said "Okay then, I'll see you when you're ready to come for a visit. Just let me know, and I'll schedule you in." Again, he nodded. I left him there on the stairs and told staff that when he was ready to come and see me just give me a call. They agreed. That was my introduction to the boy we came to know as Eli.

Eli (Elijah) came to see me about a week later. I saw him from then on every week for about a year and a half. He wanted to talk, and he talked a lot. He spoke about his family and about his foster mother. It seemed as if he didn't appreciate his foster mother when he was first sent to her, but now that he had the time to reflect on his experience, he said he would do things differently.

When he was first placed in foster care he was still reeling from the death of his biological mother and he wasn't ready to accept a surrogate. He needed time to adjust to the changes in his life, and felt that after his mother passed, the home he was living in at the time wasn't a home any longer.

From what Eli told me, his father seemed to go into a deep depression after his wife died, and it became abundantly clear that he couldn't care for Eli and his two younger siblings on his own; things just seemed to fall apart.

Now, Eli was reflecting back on his foster mother and remembered that she was a great cook and that she always provided for him. He wished he could turn back the hands of time. In retrospect, he said it was the best home he had ever had, and it was certainly better than being in residential. When asked about his own family, he said that as far back as he could remember his mother had always been sick.

Eli had started working on making puppets; he had a thing for cats and started making cats out of simple folded paper cutouts that fit over his hands. He talked about his two cats "Nag" and "Penguin."

Nag was the older of the two and the one he preferred to play with. He didn't' like to play with the other cat, Penguin, because he was a little kitten that he couldn't control, but he cared for him just the same. They seemed to have been his only friends back during that dark period of time after he lost his mother. They were a comfort to him as he identified with them in some way.

The next thing he did in art therapy was make houses for the puppet cats to live in, safe places where they could relax and be peaceful. He continued to create a safe haven for the cats that seemed to embody his wishes for his own safe place. He made them comfortable in their little cat houses with food and water, in much the same way he wanted, to be cared for.

After a few months Eli was getting used to being in the art room with me; he felt comfortable and relaxed there. He felt as if nothing bad would ever happen to him when he was within the confines of the bungalow that was known to all as the "Studio". He could talk about his past, which seemed to be the very thing he needed to do. He was processing everything that had happened to him.

All the things that seemed so surreal back then were actual events in his life, and all those memories began to bubble up to the surface. He would rant and rave, cry and talk incessantly in session about everything. He was finally letting it all out. He seemed to be thriving on the one-on-one attention and he hardly ever missed a session with me. The only time he didn't come to see me was when he had a sibling visit. Those visits were the most important days of his life.

We were told by his social worker that his dad was giving up his rights to all three children. The two younger ones were being adopted by a family. This seemed to be a double rejection for Eli, first by his father and then by this family. But Eli had other issues; he didn't want anyone else raising his little brother and sister. He resented someone else stepping in and made it difficult for them to include him in this new family structure. He was left feeling sorry for himself.

Eli spent a lot of time alone. I made the suggestion that he be in a group so that he could start to socialize and develop peer relations. He said he didn't like people and just wanted to stay in the one-on-one setting, yet he couldn't look at me when he talked, and I had to constantly remind him to look at the person he was addressing.

I informed him that it would be hard to make friends with anyone if he didn't address them by their name and look at them when he talked to them. He said he was shy, he had no confidence in his social skills and he didn't trust anyone.

It was amazing to me, that he opened up to me at all. I was as non-threatening as I could be, and, most of the time, I just listened to him. He had been through a lot. He was physically abused by his father and lost his mom. His siblings were taken from him, and he had lost his home; of course he felt that he had no power.

Looking at the world through his eyes, you could see why he didn't trust anyone, but he had to try nonetheless. He had to reach out and try to adjust to his new surroundings. Otherwise, I feared he would be destined to be alone forever.

When you hear these traumatic stories; one needs to ask the question where did it all begin? I watched an interview the other night on Piers Morgan with film producer, actor Tyler Perry. He is a fascinating personality who has dealt with his own demons; he was very candid on the show when asked about his relationship with his father.

He said their relationship had always been difficult. As a child, he had experienced brutal beating, by his hand, which weren't warranted, causing him to feel betrayed by him. As he became an adult, he wanted to know more about his dad and try to understand why he had been so brutal to him. He never had a conversation with his dad about it, but spoke with other family members about it to try and find out about his dad's childhood looking for a possible explanation for the way he treated him.

He dug around until he found out that his father was born to a slave girl down South who died giving birth to him (his dad). He then was handed off to another young girl relative (cousin), who was a mere 16 year old. She was ordered to raise Tyler's dad and his two siblings. In order for her to maintain control she used to put the children in burlap bags and string them up in a tree and beat them with a whip until they were submissive. She said she didn't have time to be fussin' over them and they just had to be quiet and do as they were told.

You can imagine the long-term effect this had on Tyler's dad who was never shown any kindness or affection growing up. All he learned to do was work, and he was a very hard worker, which was the one attribute he passed on to his son Tyler. All of his suppressed anger came out on his own children with no idea of how to relate to them in a fatherly way.

It's no wonder Mr. Perry Sr. had no skills to interact with his children after having experienced such a depraved indifference to human life. This explanation doesn't excuse or make up for what he did, but it does explain a lot about his learned behavior.

When I am working with young African Americans I often wonder about their heritage and what sort of stories maybe encoded in there familial psyche. Ancestral heritage is something that cannot be denied; we all carry imprints from our families of origin.

You don't have to go too far back in our American history to find atrocities of untold proportions. It's funny how the history books don't really dwell on the details of what really happened to the Native Americans who lived here for thousands of years before the white men came. It seems as if the history books boast about how the West was won. Even our movies show the Natives as heathens, barbarians that needed to be quelled. It is only in recent times that we have gotten the story, the full story from both sides of what really happened.

Then we need to look at the slave trade which only ended 150 years ago. I am sure many of us have ancestors who fought in the Civil War or who were plantation owners who owned and traded slaves. These imprints are part of our collective memory in the United States. You don't have to go too far back to find it, as in Tyler Perry's case his father was still born to a slave girl even though slavery was outlawed in the south long ago. It is interesting to find that there were still slaves here in the early 1900's, fifty years after the end of slavery. Yet we know that the slave trade is alive and well in the world and young girls are sold into the sex slave trade every day.

The interesting part of Tyler's story is that he said the Buck stops here with me. He made a conscious effort to not carry on the legacy.

When a young child comes to me and asks, "Why do I have to live in foster care? Why was I abandoned by my family?" You probably don't have to go too far back in their family history to find the root cause. How many families were torn apart by the slave trade, civil war or religious persecution? How many babies were born in disgrace and degradation? How many generations does a family need to experience this sort of uprooting, learned helplessness, and downright lack of human dignity being forced upon them until they start to believe it?

These feelings and memories are encoded into the fiber of the ancestral cellular memory. The experiences of trauma are handed down to their offspring who inherit the impression. In order to find solutions you have to be consciously aware of your history. Often times these learned experiences are handed down from generation to generation. Causing recipients of negative thought patterns to seek solutions that will make them feel better about themselves (Woolger, 1988). That may work in the short run but overtime this kind of intervention doesn't hold up and is maladaptive to the outside world.

Anger can be a learned behavior that's been handed down for generations from experiences of unresolved retribution. Offspring can also fall into hopelessness and despair where drugs and alcohol are the only relief. This is why I feel it is imperative to incorporate family constellation work and family analyses into therapy. This is the only way to break the repetitious patterns of feelings of unworthiness, being unloved, or unwanted. If you want the patterns to shift you have to address them head on and recognize the familial carry-overs in your blood line.

In the case of Eli, I felt he had a lot of carryovers from his familial past that needed to be understood. The problem was that he didn't know his family, and he had no connection to them.

Whenever I asked him, "Where was your mother born or what where your grandparents like?" He would say he didn't know. It seems as if he lived in a vacuum, with no outside stimuli. He didn't know his aunts and uncles, and had no memory of ever interacting with his grandparents.

I found this startling but not uncommon for children in foster care or group homes. They have been displaced in the family line for a very long time, and their parents may have been displaced as well, so it is hard to reconstruct the family of origin because it has been splintered for so long.

Perhaps that is why he was so determined to hold on to his siblings, and I was happy to see that the agency went to great lengths to have them meet weekly. Keeping his siblings together and pursuing his studies were the two areas that I could help nurture as a way out of his very dire situation.

The more time he spent in therapy, the more Eli began to come out of his shell. He was smart and did well in school. This was the one area in his life that he could excel in, and he was encouraged by his staff, his social worker, and by me to continue with his studies.

We all knew this was one way to build up Eli's sense of self and start to feel good again living with a sense of purpose. The best medicine for Eli was to get an A on a test. It fed his ego and built up his confidence. He would bring homework with him into session and we would work on it together. He was very proud of his grades.

However, a lot of the time Eli came to session and spent the whole hour ranting and spewing venomous talk, not at me particularly; he just wanted to hear himself talk about the injustices he had been through. It was like vomit that just kept coming up.

I asked him to draw me a picture of a person, not anyone in particular, just a figure, as full a figure as he could draw. He drew a boy with no hands and no feet.

I said, "There are no feet on this person. How can he move if he has no feet"?

Eli replied, "Exactly. That is why I am struck in this hell hole."

"Okay, I see you feel stuck, and you have no hands either. Do you feel as if you have no control over your life?"

"I don't. I have no control over anything."

"So is that why you get so angry, because you feel as if you have no control over anything?"

"Yeah, that's right. I get mad."

"Is that what happened to you the other day? You got mad and had to be restrained at your house?"

"I got mad because I had a flashback."

"I see; a flashback to when?"

"When I was twelve."

"When you were 12, are you sure? That was a long time ago. You remember that you were exactly twelve?"

"Yeah, I remember."

"That was four years ago. You remember when you were twelve? Are you sure?"

"I told you I'm sure."

"Well, what happened? Do you want to talk about when you were twelve?"

"I don't want to talk about it."

"Okay, well maybe you can draw me a picture about what happened."

"Oh, I hate this. I can't draw."

"Okay, I understand. You don't want to draw it. Perhaps I can draw a picture for you? I know this is hard, but you get angry when you remember this. You feel it. Where do you feel it?"

"In my head."

"Okay, what color is it in your head?"

"Red."

"Great! Okay, like this?" I drew a red head.

"Yeah, like that. It pounds and bulges and pulsates in my head."

"So you get angry when you get this flashback and it starts pounding in your head?"

"Yeah, I get migraines."

"So you get migraines in your head?"

"Yes, I get migraines."

"So the first time this happened, when you got this migraine, you were twelve? You're sure you remember?"

"Yes, I'm sure, my mother died when I was twelve. I remember!"

"So when you think about that day, the day your mother died, you get a migraine?"

"Yeah, I get a pounding, pulsating, migraine."

"You act as if it was a surprise the day your mother died. You told me she was sick for a long time, so you must have known that day would come. Yet when the day finally came, you were surprised?"

"I didn't know it was going to happen then on that day. God she got me so mad. I always told her to take her medicine (crying). She didn't always take it. I told her to never forget. She didn't listen to me."

"So you felt helpless. You couldn't make her take it, and you couldn't make her better; you couldn't help her."

"No, I couldn't help her (crying). She died anyway."

"So, now, when you think about it, you get angry because you couldn't help her and she didn't listen to you."

"No, I couldn't make her take it."

"Eli taking a pill doesn't always cure the illness. Even if she took her medicine it was only to help her get through it. It wasn't your fault that she got sick. And even if she took her medicine it wasn't a guarantee. Do you understand that?"

"I know, but she's gone, and I can't bring her back, and my head hurts when I think about it."

"What makes the pain go away?"

"Sweets! Candy makes it go away."

"Candy!" I said with surprise.

Eli smiled. "Yeah, candy."

So I reached into my desk where I have some M & M's and I said, "Here, you can have some of these." He smiled and began eating the candies. "So are you feeling better now?" I asked.

"Yes, thank you."

"So when you get sweets you feel better. What else is sweet?"

"My mother, she was sweet. She was sweet to me."

"So, now, when you have sweets you think about how sweet your mother was to you, and you feel better."

"Yeah, when people are sweet to me the way she was sweet to me, when people are nice to me, the pain goes away."

At this point I was completely drained. I couldn't bring her back, so, now, I was feeling hopeless. People die; people you love die. It's sad, but it happens. The problem was there was no one else to take care of Eli and his siblings when she died. And it seemed like his dad took all his anger out on them. All of his frustration went into them, so they couldn't stay with him; they had to leave.

That was when their situation went from bad to worse. Eli was only twelve, his brother was about ten and his sister was even younger. Eli felt responsible for them; he felt responsible for his mother, and he was only twelve. But he needed to move on. It wasn't his fault. He needed to find the sweetness in life. He was right about that.

I could feel his emptiness. He had lost everything. Now all he wanted was to get his brother and sister back. Eli became obsessed with wanting to get out on his own. He had decided that he was going to sign himself out when he was eighteen, get a job, get married, and take in his two siblings. He was a good big brother, but he lacked a real plan on how he would accomplish his goal. I didn't want to discourage him from having a dream, but he needed a realistic plan to have it become a reality. He had no skills, no work experience.

There was only one way he could make this work, and that was to stay in school and get grades that would help him get into college. Even if he were to go to a two-year school or job core, that would take him one step closer to attaining his dream. He could study something like computer programming that I thought was realistic.

Most of our sessions together centered on reality testing. He could hold the bigger picture in his mind while accomplishing smaller goals that were attainable for him to reach at his age and at his developmental level. This objective was very hard for Elijah. He felt as if he had no real skills and that no one would hire him. He said that when his mother died he died too, that the only thing that made him feel alive was when he was with a girl. He desperately wanted to have a girlfriend that he could love and be loved by. This became his sole objective. He felt alone and wanted desperately to have someone special in his life.

There was little opportunity for Elijah to meet girls. He had no free time off campus and there were no girls in his school. This was part of his frustration. He said it wasn't normal for teenage boys to be cooped up in a place where they couldn't meet girls. He wanted to have a normal high school experience. I couldn't blame him for feeling the way that he did; he needed to get out into the community more. I made a recommendation for Elijah to get into an after-school program in the community. By doing this, he could at least be more sociable.

This afterschool opportunity was perfect for Eli. He could get out into the community, meet other kids, and learn some valuable skills such as money management, resume writing, career planning, and social skills. This program gave him hope; he went every week, never missing a chance to meet girls, and he was starting to socialize.

I kept seeing Eli once a week, but also started him in a dyad with Lamar. They both needed to connect with a peer they could trust, someone that they could develop a lasting friendship with. The dyad started off slowly. It was mostly a venting session for Elijah to act out with an audience, and it didn't take much for Lamar to get sucked into his venomous negativity.

Finally, I got the boys to work together by creating some life sized drawings of each other. The day I started this project was not a good day for Eli. He was in a foul mood and he didn't want to do it. He had just come back from a sibling visit and passed the cemetery where his mother was buried. This sent him into a tirade about his mother's funeral. He needed to process his feelings about that day.

All he wanted to do was to curse out everyone. He used the worst, angriest words he could think of. He cursed out just about everyone who went to the funeral and then started in on his dad, who had not attended. He became very animated, pacing up and down the room and waving his arms.

Lamar just sat there shaking his head. Eli looked over at him and said, "What's your problem?" Lamar said, "Well at least your mother is at peace now that she is dead. My mother might as well be dead. I'll never see her so she is dead to me anyway." Elijah retorted, "Well, at least you have a mother."

This was the first time Elijah took pause and for a moment and thought about someone else's pain. He knew immediately the living hell that Lamar was going through. Imagine having a mother who was presumably so preoccupied with her own drug addiction; she didn't even have time for her own son. How frustrating was if for him to be in this situation?

In some way it's easier when a person dies; you can bury them and move on. But Lamar couldn't do that; he was stuck in limbo.

Elijah didn't want to move on because being attached to his mother's memory was all he had, and the pain of losing her was what he hung on to. Elijah looked at Lamar as if he was seeing him for the first time and realized he was not the only one dealing with a loss.

I jumped in at this point and said "Hold on to those feelings you have right now. I want you to think about how those feelings sit inside of you. Draw your heart inside of the figure, drawing just the way you are feeling right now. Okay Eli, Lamar, you got it? Let's do this!"

I tried to get Elijah involved, but he just scribbled on his paper. Lamar, on the other hand, drew a large outline of a figure with a huge heart in the chest. His heart was cut up into many parts: joy, sadness, love, anger and one empty space, which needed to be filled.

The empty space seemed to represent the empty hole that was left in his heart where his mother used to be. Elijah could not access his hurt; he didn't want to, but, at least, he tolerated Lamar's attempts. Perhaps Lamar's influence in trying to process his feelings would prompt Elijah to do the same.

The hurt, for Eli, was so deep he could lose himself in it. He was afraid of that. Death was very real to Eli, and I think he was afraid that feeling and reliving the memory of his mother's death was pulling him into death itself.

The real truth of the matter was that Eli didn't want to die. Yes, a part of him died when his mother died; he said that, but there was another part that was very much alive. What he held onto was the pain of her death because he felt close to her. He also had the guilt of wanting or having a life while his mom was dead.

Lamar, on the other hand, could connect with his feelings. He wanted to understand what happened to him and he wanted to fix what was wrong. Even if he could fix his confusion or his anger, he needed to understand that he couldn't fix, his mom. Either way, he didn't want to stay in limbo. He wanted to change his situation, he didn't' want to be stuck. He had the courage to try to change it, where Eli was stuck in the guilt, one of the hardest emotions to change.

The atmosphere in the room was heavy and thick. I needed to change their fixed states, and movement was the best cure for that. The weather was starting to get nice, so I took the two boys outside to enjoy some springtime activity.

Lamar wanted to play stick ball. I hadn't played stick ball since I was a kid but I needed to connect with these boys and I needed them to connect with each other, so I had to go the distance with them. It wasn't art, but it was a way to get them to relate to each other.

Lamar was all about the game, but as par for the course, Eli didn't want to play (feeling helpless). He said he didn't like sports, he wasn't good at them, and didn't want to be laughed at. Lamar, however, was very caring toward Eli. He told him, "Look, this isn't a contest. There's nothing to win. We just want to fool around and have some fun."

Eli was still reluctant, and kept insisting that he couldn't do it. I said, "Look, Eli, if you think I can do this, you're really kidding yourself. I'm no athlete, and I haven't played in maybe twenty years. But I don't care if I look silly. If I can do it so can you. Come on, we can't play without you."

At this point Lamar pretended to be a sportscaster, saying things like "The slugger is coming to bat. The pitch is high. He swings, and it's a foul ball." It was funny, and it added momentum to the game.

Eli finally came to bat, hit the ball high in the air, and it was going, going gone, a home run. Eli flew around the bases and you could almost hear the roar of the crowd. It was so funny even Eli had to laugh. We played round robin so everyone got a turn to pitch and to hit. It was a lot of fun, and the boys really had a good time. At the end of the hour, I was getting tired so I suggested we all go out for a soda and ice cream. They really loved that.

So I got the boys to bond a little and forget they were in placement for now. They were just two boys having a good time. Life is too short to always be focused on what went wrong or what happened in the past. Playing sports, in particular, was a great way to be in the moment and just be yourself and have fun. This was truly a bonding experience.

The next time we got together, it was Lamar's birthday. I decided to take the boys to the park. We talked about birthdays, along with some of their fondest memories relating to their birthdays.

Lamar remembered a birthday in which his whole family was together. They went to a park just like the one we were in, where they barbequed and had a really good time. Eli remembered going to the very same park we were in with his foster family. They were happy times, the times you needed to hang onto when you were down in the dumps.

I wanted to give the boys some good, happy memories about their time together, reiterating that it was up to them from here on in to make good times for themselves. I told them their future hadn't been written yet. They could write whatever story they wanted to.

By this time, the boys were becoming more familiar with each other. Eli wasn't barking like a dog anymore, and he had a friend in the house that he could talk to, so he wasn't feeling so alone. Lamar was a realist with an optimistic bent, while Eli was walking around with a dark cloud over his head. He epitomized true victim consciousness. I thought that perhaps they could balance each other out.

One particularly interesting session occurred when I asked the boys to create a piece around the topic of friendship. To start, Lamar took a piece of torn blue paper and glued it down on a piece of 12" x 18" white paper. He said blue was the color of "True Blue."

Then I asked Lamar if Eli could add something to his piece of art. Eli added two strips of green paper and one strip of yellow. Lamar then added a crumpled up piece of white paper on the other side of the paper. They were then asked to write something about friendship. Lamar wrote "Love, caring, and having fun." Eli wrote "Honesty, truthfulness, being nice, and no ignoring."

Then it came time to write a title for the piece. Eli wrote, "I like peace," while Lamar wrote, "A good friend knows how to have fun." This seemed to outline for each boy what his criteria was for a good relationship. Eli needed trust and always being there for the other. For Lamar, a buddy to hang out with, to have fun with, and to be able to just be himself with seemed most important. This was a big step for the both of them. Time would tell if they could supply the necessary ingredients to build a lasting relationship. But, for now, I think they had mutual respect for each other.

Despair to Resiliency

$\mathcal{L}$AMAR HAD MANY LOSSES over the years, and I think that when we said goodbye to Alessandro, he felt like he was losing a friend; just add one more loss to the list. That is why I thought introducing him to Eli was a good idea. After he had drawn the knight and wolf story, I knew friendship was very important to him.

Another interesting picture he drew was that of a boy standing guard at night with a sword in his hand. In the distance was a house. It was all broken down with boarded up windows, but he stood there nevertheless, because it was his home, and he was going to defend it. He was not about to give up on his dream of having a home.

I remember when one of the boys in the group didn't want to make his mother a Mother's Day card, Lamar said to me in private, "He'll be sorry one day. You have only one mother. You can't turn your back on her because if it wasn't for her, you wouldn't be here."

I told Lamar it's a good thing to recognize the important role your mother plays in your life, but sometimes I think some women aren't the mothering type. I felt that some women were instruments for bringing children into the world but weren't necessarily meant to raise them. This was a difficult concept for a boy so young to grasp but I didn't want Lamar to hope beyond what was realistic.

There was another instance in which Lamar played with the Legos. He built a bridge, and, no, matter how many times that bridge fell down Lamar would always build it back up. For someone who had a low tolerance level, who was impulsive, and extremely ADD, he always had the patience and resilience to rebuild that bridge, over and over again. He never had patience with anything else but demonstrated incredible fortitude with that bridge.

We talked about the bridge and its symbolic meaning. The bridge, he said, connected him to his mother. I was happy that he could understand the meaning behind his creations. In a way, it was the dream that connected him because he was never going to give up on it.

He had been in placement for about two years now, and he was still hoping to get discharged back to his home. His mother had been in rehab for most of the time that Lamar had been in residential. Now that she was on her own we would see if she would come around, this was the real test.

As time went on, Lamar was acting out more and more. His tolerance was wearing thin, and he was like a time bomb to the staff. As it turned out his mother hardly ever called him and never came to visit. I think that was the hardest part, not knowing what she was doing or where she was.

Lamar was getting angry about it. He had been such a devoted warrior, but twenty-four months was a long time for a boy of thirteen; it must have felt like a lifetime.

He started drawing pictures of a crazy deranged woman smoking crack. He said he hated her because she loved her crack more that she loved him.

Lamar said, "She always tells me she is going to stop but she never does."

So the question needed to be asked, "Lamar, do you think she can stop?"

He replied, "No, she doesn't want to stop." He then told me, "When she was high, she would send me outside to play. She spent all of her money on crack, and she even took my clothes and shoes and sold them to buy it. She once stole my friend's jacket to buy crack. That is why I stopped bringing friends home to my house."

I replied "So what you are telling me, Lamar, is that this has been going on for a long time. You have been such a brave boy waiting here holding on, hoping for this nightmare to end. I've seen you, and I know. I have great respect for you Lamar. I know you want to do the right thing. But what do you need, what do you want for yourself? Do you ever think about what you want instead of what you feel is your duty to do and to uphold?"

Lamar was shaking his head and saying, "I know. I know."

"So what do you want, Lamar?"

"I want to be adopted by someone else!"

"That's it, that's what you want?"

"Yes that's what I want."

"How do you feel now that you have made this decision?"

"I'm very sad about it."

"I know you are Lamar. I can feel that you are sad about it. Does this mean that you don't love your mother anymore?"

"No, no, Ms. G. I still love my mother. I will always love my mother."

"That's right, Lamar. You will always love your mother. No one can ever take that away from you. That you will always have. But what this means is that you love yourself and that you need certain things for yourself that she can't give you right now. You will always be her son, and you will always love her. But this is about what you need. So what are some of the things you need? Can you write a list?"

"Number one, I want decent clothes. Two, I want someone to care about me. Three, I want someone I can look up to. And four, I want someone who is truthful, who follows through on what they say they are going to do."

This was the first time Lamar thought about what he wanted instead of what his mother needed. He was very sad. He looked so defeated, as if he had lost the war, and he seemed so hurt.

I walked him back to his house and gave him a big hug. I told him he was very brave, that this may be the most difficult decision he may ever have to make; he needed a real home and family. He deserved to have that because he was a great kid who deserved to have a life that was happy, and secure. He was in such a dilemma. If his mother didn't love herself enough to save herself, how would she ever be able to love Lamar, and if Lamar loved himself enough to want to have a life then he felt guilty.

Later that day, he needed to be restrained at the house and was sent to the "Crisis Unit." This was a confined locked facility where he would be watched twenty-four hours a day, so that he wouldn't hurt himself or anyone else.

I didn't see him for a few weeks after that. He needed to adjust to the new perspective he had on his life; this was a reality that was hard for him to accept.

When he returned to art therapy, he seemed to have a fresh outlook. He started making a cross, saying that if there was a decision that needed to be made, Jesus would help him make it. The cross also represented the cross that he had to bear in life.

The dilemma Lamar was facing was the feeling that he had let his mother down, instead of her letting him down. Now, on top of feeling guilty, he had this overwhelming feeling that he was a bad son. He was bad and needed to be punished. This is not unusual for a boy who didn't want to believe that his parent was bad and needed to learn how to be responsible. He was taking the blame because if he felt his mother was at fault then there would be no hope. He was still holding out the hope in his heart that she was the "good mother" who loved him.

Lamar was also thinking at this time that perhaps his baby brother's foster mother would take him as well. And so the agency started sibling visits in the hope that he could possibly have a visiting resource. He started visiting on weekends and then moved into weekend overnight visits.

This development was very temporary, however, as Lamar became jealous of the younger brother. The foster mother found Lamar to be unpredictable; he acted out to get all of the attention, and he proved to be too difficult for her to handle. Lamar fell hard after this; he became despondent and even more angry. Lamar was a great kid when he had all of your attention on a one-to-one basis, but put him in a room with other kids and it was a whole different ball game.

Boundaries needed to be maintained, not only for order in the classroom but in order to protect him and the other kids. In session, we spent a lot of time talking about these topics, and there were boundaries set up in the art room as well, boundaries for what conduct was to be followed, for safety reasons, for general maintenance of the supplies, etcetera. Intellectually, Lamar knew why boundaries were necessary, but emotionally he couldn't follow through with what he needed to do.

Lamar had done a painting from a directive which I asked him to paint. A landscape with him in it, the kind of landscape that he felt he was in presently. He painted a chicken in a barren setting. This chicken was walking down the road until it came to a fork in it. Evidently, this chicken had stopped at the intersection and couldn't decide which way to go. Lamar said if he went one way, he would get shelter, food, friends, and more. If he went the other way, he got nothing; he was on his own. Yet he stands there in the middle unable to move. He said if he goes to the right he is being selfish and is only thinking of himself.

That is where the guilt came in. "If I get everything, I need and I'm taken care of, but my mom is alone with nothing on the other side, what's the point of that?" That is what he was thinking.

I didn't think he was being selfish. I thought he was being realistic. Even if he did go to the left to be with his mom she could potentially hurt him again, physically and emotionally. Yet he was willing to risk it all just to be with her.

Now that he was getting older, he thought he would be able to handle the ups and downs of her mood swings, and, physically, he was bigger and stronger, thinking that he could defend himself. But as long as she was still using drugs, the court would never allow him to go home. Every time she would go into rehab, he became hopeful that she would be able to turn it around.

Meanwhile, he was still in limbo, and as long as he was in limbo, he could only survive if he adopted an "I don't care" attitude. As hard as I tried to get him motivated, he would start projects and leave them unfinished. His hygiene was declining, he wasn't trying in school, and his grades were failing. He didn't seem to care about anything, not even himself.

All the therapy in the world was not helping him to feel worthy. He felt that he was damaged goods and no one wanted him, because the reality of the situation was that nothing changed. Deep down Lamar felt that if his mother didn't love him then no one else would love him either. This was a catch 22; for as long as he believed that, then he would not present himself in a way that would make it easy for someone else to love him. If he could learn to care about himself he would seem more attractive to a prospective family.

His mother was apparently still using and not visiting him. There were no families out there that wanted him and he was stuck in a residential program that he felt was keeping him away from his family. No matter how much the staff and the therapists tried to boost his ego and self-confidence, it never stuck. It was nothing compared to what one phone call from his mother would do.

In order for Lamar to be adopted he would have to completely reject his mother. That would be the only way he would be able to be part of a real family. His mother's rights would have to be terminated.

I felt that all I was doing was helping him pass the time until something significant happened that would change his situation. The relationship I tried to develop between the two boys, Lamar and Eli, also had its ups and downs. They would run hot and cold; they would fight and sometimes not want to be in each other's company. Yet there was one small ray of sunshine that offered the boys some hope, a summer activity that seemed to lift their spirits.

There was a plan for the boys to go away on a camping trip for a week. They both knew there would be girls at this camp and they were very excited about it. This was the boost Lamar needed to take his mind off of his quandary.

In the art room it was hard to contain the boy's enthusiasm about being with girls for a whole week. As we got closer to the time of their departure, they became more and more hyper. All Eli could talk about was having sex with the first girl he saw. He was desperate for a relationship and the attention a girlfriend would give him. I was fearful that he would get involved with the first girl that said hello to him. But then again he might not get a hello from anyone. Lamar was a little bit more reserved.

I for one didn't know how staff would be able to control these boys around the girls, and I was glad I wasn't asked to chaperone them. But the trip was the highlight of their summer, and it gave them something else to think about instead of their desperate situations. So off they went for a week of fun in the sun with a bunch of other kids, with activities galore to take their minds off their troubles.

When they returned to campus after the week was over, they were full of stories. They both seemed to have had a really good time, and Eli did manage to get a few phone numbers out of the deal. That was enough to keep him content for quite some time.

While at camp Eli had time to reflect on his situation and he now realized that it was his mother who kept his family together. She worked, paid the bills and disciplined the kids; basically she did everything. His dad didn't work; he did drugs and virtually caused all of the family's problems. He was so angry with his dad right now because he realized it was his mom who he owed everything to. Since she was gone, the whole family fell apart.

It was partly because his mom was incredibly strong that Eli wanted a girlfriend so badly. In his mind, it seemed as though it was the woman who was the one in the relationship that kept it together, and the guy was just a screw—up, like him. He seemed to think that the only way he would straighten out his situation was if he found a good, loving, hard-working woman to make everything right. His psyche was hardwired to find a girl to help keep him together the way his mom kept him together. After all this time of reflection on his family's situation, he came to the conclusion that he didn't want anything to do with his dad.

It was hard for me to work with Eli because he had no outside interests. He didn't like sports, he wasn't social with the other boys, he didn't like to do art, and he was as stubborn as the day was long. The only things he was interested in were school, video games, girls, and visiting with his brother and sister. The one real joy he had was the time spent visiting with his siblings at their foster mother's home. He was very anxious about these visits, and he always looked forward to the time spent with them off campus.

Lamar, on the other hand, was getting so anxious about his situation that he went AWOL. He went missing for about ten days until the authorities found him and brought him back. He was back in the crisis center again and down on his luck.

My suspicion was that he went looking for his mom; since she didn't call him or visit with him, he took matters into his own hands. As dangerous as it was being out on the street alone, didn't seem to matter he was willing to risk everything to find her. He just couldn't sit and wait any longer. He needed to see her and hear from her what was really going on. He could not and would not follow through on any decision without seeing her first.

Working Through the Catharsis

SHANE CONTINUED TO COME to art therapy as usual but there seemed to be a change in Shane's demeanor, a shift in the way he thought about himself. He was starting to become his own person. Oddly enough, there was no mention of his dad after the day he had faced his ghost and his deepest fears about him. I felt that he had finally buried him, and there was no need to bring him back from the dead, I certainly wasn't going to bring it up.

Instead, Shane focused his attention on his mother. She had always been there for him in some way but her physical disability did not allow her the opportunity to keep him home. He seemed to understand that she wanted to be there for him but was limited. She kept his bedroom at her home where he could visit her on weekends and now that he was getting better he was visiting more and more often.

We all started to see great changes in Shane toward the end of the school year. He started to come out of his self-imposed isolation. He was more social, he started getting really good grades in school and he even made the honor roll. He was taking better care of himself, showering daily, and taking an interest in the clothes he wore and how he looked and his medication was greatly reduced. He started spending more time off campus, and I was wondering if he was getting too much freedom too soon.

Things seemed to be going well for Shane. He was taking an interest in landscape painting, so I took him to the park by the river to paint. I'll never forget one day when we were there painting. He started painting a dock that went out into the river.

There was perspective involved and reflections from the deck on the water that sort of challenged him, so he asked me for some help.

I simply added some darks and reflected light to the surface of the water, and explained to him why I added the complimentary colors that I used. He absorbed the information like a sponge. He could understand the principle behind it and loved the realism that developed before his eyes. He took the paints and brushes and continued on his own for awhile. Then I took a look and could see that the painting really started to come together.

I said, "There you go Shane. Now you've got it". He jumped up and gave me a bear hug and said with complete joy, "Thank you, Ms. G. Thank you so much for helping me believe in myself."

I was stunned. I hadn't expected this to happen and it brought tears to my eyes because I never realized that he would think to give me credit for anything he was doing. This was one of those precious moments that made my job worthwhile.

Shane completed the painting and added it to his portfolio, as he had expressed an interest in going on to art school. We discussed his future plans many times, and he knew he wanted to go on for further study in the arts, but he felt responsible for his mom and didn't want to go too far from where she lived.

Fortunately, Shane happened to be in the right place, because there were many very good art schools in the area, a stone's throw from where his mother lived. He felt encouraged by this, and I thought, "What a good son to be so concerned for his mother's well-being." It was a double-edged sword though, because it was also a tremendous burden for such a young boy to even think about taking on such a responsibility.

Shane kept coming to art therapy, but I started to see another change in him. At first, I thought it was because they had reduced his meds to the point where he was hardly taking anything. That was a miracle in itself, since this boy had been heavily medicated since he was about five years old. But it turned out the change I was seeing was steeped in something way more sinister.

Shane exhibited moodiness, rebellious outbursts in the art room (where he didn't want me to suggest anything); he suddenly seemed to think that he knew everything. In other words, he was turning into a typical, full-blown teenager.

I was beginning to think I had created a monster. He went from an innocent five-year-old to a rebellious fifteen-year-old, seemingly overnight. He started questioning authority and didn't want to talk to me any longer. He seemed to try and hide things from me and was afraid that I wouldn't approve of whatever he was doing on the outside. He didn't trust me any longer.

His drawings started to change as well. He was now drawing pictures of boys with bandanas on their heads and chains around their necks. I was beginning to see signs of gang affiliation and I knew Shane was entering into an area he knew nothing about. He didn't have any screening mechanisms to detect the street kid's manipulative motives for their interest in him. He wanted so desperately to be accepted by his peers he would have done anything to be part of the "in crowd," even if that meant being part of a gang. And he certainly didn't want me to know about it, because he didn't want to be judged by me. He thought the sun rose and set on those gang kids.

The next thing I knew Shane was starting to get into trouble. He went from a model resident who had made a complete 360° turnaround to a juvenile delinquent with a police record. Evidently, he had to do something illegal to be accepted into the gang, and he fell prey to their manipulation and greed. He was charged and sent to a juvenile detention center.

I was crushed. I wished for the innocent little boy to come back into session with me. I knew he was safe here at the agency. Shane was not a street kid; he was totally at the mercy of the gang.

I heard that he was in the crisis residence until the court hearing was finalized. I hadn't had a chance to say goodbye to him so I took it upon myself to go and see him there in crisis. I just wanted to tell him that we all make mistakes, that he was just trying to fit in with the wrong crowd, and that he could turn it around.

He didn't want to see me, and he looked so forlorn. I was brief. I just wanted him to know that I hadn't given up on him. I told him it wasn't the end of the world, but it was a wakeup call. He shook his head in agreement, and then I had to leave him. I knew there would be no updates for me to follow him. Once a kid was out of our jurisdiction, there was very little information available to us. I lost track of him after he left the campus.

I prayed that he would see the error in his ways and come full circle back to us. He needed to understand that the gang was just using him. I knew all he wanted was to be accepted by what he thought were cool kids, but he was way too innocent. He had no street smarts at all. He was just devoured by them.

I also knew that Shane had a deep belief in God and a strong conscience. I just think he got too much freedom too soon and didn't know what to do with it. It all happened so fast. He seemed to want to make up for lost time.

I saw Shane about a year later when he had done his time in the JD facility. He did eventually come back to the agency. This time he was on the straight and narrow. He was placed in a more independent living cottage and was out of my jurisdiction. He was working on getting his high school diploma and he still wanted to go to art school. He was happy to see me and proud to show me his sketch book. I wished him well and told him if he ever needed any help with his portfolio to call on me.

What I had seen happen many times, was the agency trying to move kids through the system. The state wanted kids to be placed back with their families of origin and out of state care, which I could understand. It was expensive to keep kids in residential, so if they saw improvements, they would make referrals toward a discharge plan.

For some it worked, but for others, it backfired. Too much freedom too soon would turn out to be a prescription for disaster on the outside. It was a fine line between success and failure and therefore needed to be judged carefully.

If a child was in the system too long, they would become dependent on it and never be able to make it on their own. If they were moved out too fast, they would fall on their faces. At some point, you have to test the waters and see if independence will work, but what I wanted to see happen was input from all of the people who worked on a case come together to make decisions about their discharge plans rather than have it come from the top.

In many cases the CEO's and social work supervisors didn't really know a kid as intimately as the line staff or therapists who worked with them every day. They never took into consideration our thoughts about a discharge plan, and, many times, they made the wrong decision. Then it was up to us to pick up the pieces.

Some children are eighteen years old chronologically but only five years old emotionally. However, kids can sign themselves out at eighteen, which is a scary thing for most. If the child doesn't have a support network on the outside, they are totally vulnerable. If they are still in high school, they can stay with us until they graduate, or until they are 21 years of age. This gives them valuable maturity time, then they can go out on their own and chances are be more successful.

As time went on, I could tell that the state didn't want to keep kids in residential longer than they had to. In a lot of cases, as soon as their parents finished their parenting classes, they would be discharged to them. And, many times, these very same kids would be in trouble and back within six months of discharge.

Unfortunately, if they got into trouble and were over eighteen, more often than not they would be sent to jail. At least this time Shane was back and moving in the right direction. I think he learned an important lesson his first time out and knew he couldn't survive the street on his own.

Between a Rock and a Hard Place

*W*HAT WOULD HAPPEN TO Lamar? I couldn't help thinking about that. He was only thirteen, and being discharged to a parent didn't look like it was a viable plan. But, until his mother's rights were terminated, he couldn't be adopted. He could however be put into a foster home.

His behavior was up and down emotionally. Each day turned into an eternity for him and his patience was wearing thin. He just couldn't hold it together any longer. I started seeing him twice a week to give him the support he needed through this difficult time.

He had managed to sabotage the possibility of going to his baby brother's foster home, and I was beginning to think he didn't want that, so it didn't appear to be an option for him. Now, he was looking at going to live with his stepdad. I knew that in the back of his mind, he wanted to live with his stepdad, in hope that eventually there would be a chance to see his mom. Even though his parents weren't together any longer, his stepdad was the closest person to her that he knew, so Lamar felt that would be his best opportunity to see her.

I didn't think it was a good idea to go back with his step-dad. I didn't know him so I couldn't say why particularly what my objection was but if he was going to be pulled back into a crag mire of difficult choices I didn't think it was a good idea. I wished he could make a clean break of it and go with a whole new family, one that would be a positive influence on him and get him away from the reminders of the past.

I asked him several times, if he could see himself in a different family, what kind a family would it be? What he described was going home with me. I was truly touched but had to be honest with him. As much as I cared about him and wanted to do the right thing for him, it would be unethical for me to do that. I said to him, "Lamar what about all the other kids? If I were to take you home how do you think they would all feel? I would be letting them down and then they would be jealous of you. Besides, don't you want a younger mother? I would be more like a grandmother to you. I think a younger family that you could grow with would be a better idea, don't you?"

He seemed very forlorn. He couldn't share a mother with anyone else; he needed to have all of the attention; that was the problem. Families were hard to find, especially for a kid with special needs.

For the next six months all of us at the agency tried to help Lamar hold it together. Then, in February, while Lamar was back in the Crisis Residence, I went to see him there. He wanted to make a Valentine's Day card for his mother. In the card, he wrote that he wished her a happy Valentine's Day but went on to say that he was afraid that she would fall back into her old ways, and he said he didn't feel it would be safe for him to move back with her. Therefore, he had decided that he didn't want to live with her anymore.

I was relieved to see this and asked him if he was sure that this was the message he wanted to send to her. He was sure but so sad. He really looked like he just lost the last hope in the world for ever having the family he wanted.

But, at last, he finally made a decision. For three years, he had been tormented with this, sitting on the fence, not being able to move on with his life, and feeling like the worst son in the world. But, today, he wrote it in a card, and he signed it. He wanted to mail it to her. He wanted her to know that he had finally made a decision. I had mixed emotions about the whole thing. I knew it was the right thing for Lamar to do, I just wished he didn't have to suffer so much.

It's like when you have a terminally ill parent on life support that has a living will, and you're the only child that has to make the decision as to whether or not to pull the plug. You finally make the decision to pull it, and your parent dies. You are left feeling responsible for their death, but, at the same time, you are relieved they are not suffering any longer.

Two weeks later, he had a service plan review and neither of his parents showed up for it. He was devastated beyond anyone's imagination. He took the blame for it, saying that it was his fault. He was bad, and they didn't want to have anything to do with him. He became suicidal after that day and had to be placed on twenty-four-hour surveillance. I thought about Eli and how his mother had passed away, and so, in some way, he was free to think about himself and move on. But this was not the case for Lamar.

After the Valentine's Day card was made it went to the court as a legal document. That signature was all they needed to start proceedings against his mother, and it was presented at the next court hearing.

That started the ball rolling for his mother's rights to be terminated. After all the torment that this poor boy had been through, the next time he came to the art room, he made it very clear that he was feeling guilty. He made a huge poster with burning fire and words engulfed in flames that said, "Through the fires of burning hell, I still love you."

Sabotage

$\mathcal{E}$LI HAD STARTED SPENDING more and more time with his siblings' foster family. The agency was testing the waters to see if he could be reunited permanently with them. He knew that this was his last hope at having a family, and he was on his best behavior.

The first few visits seemed to go fairly well. Then the trouble started. Evidently, he felt that he should have the final word on how to discipline his brother and sister. He didn't like the way the foster mother spoke to them or treated them. And so a conflict arose in which he was trying to redefine the rules of the house, and this was not taken lightly by the foster mom.

In the end, it was decided that this family would not plan for Eli at all. They didn't even want him coming to visit there in that house, and so all the visits had to be made at a neutral location. This, of course, shattered his dreams of being reunited with his siblings. He said he felt like a dog that had been kicked around because no one wanted it.

What I felt was happening was that Eli had had so much loss in his life that he set himself up for failure. He didn't believe that he could be happy or that he deserved to have a family. Remember, on some level, he felt responsible for his mother's death. So how could he have happiness after that? He seemed to be sabotaging any other outcome. He didn't think happiness was really possible.

However, all change starts with what you believe in. My job therefore was to help him change the premise that he did deserve to have happiness. It was difficult for me to get him to wrap his brain around the fact the he had to start thinking differently in order to change his situation. His attitude pushed people away, and his anti-social behavior didn't allow for anyone to get close to him. He hid himself away inside video games so that he wouldn't be rejected by anyone. Then when he tried to re-adapt, as in the case with his siblings' foster family, it backfired.

He couldn't control his angry outbursts, and this foster mother couldn't have him undermining her ability to discipline the younger children. Eli would certainly not listen to her, as he felt he was the man in charge. He also had the added pressure of having promised his mother on her deathbed that he would keep the family together. This was his driving motivation, to keep the promise he made to his mother.

Eli lost his mother, he lost his home, he lost his brother and sister, and he almost lost his mind. He had lost his control over his emotions, so he went to the only logical place (inside). He felt that was the way to insulate himself from the outside world or from any further loss. He felt that a video game would be the safest place to hide.

Now that being re-united with his siblings was out of the question, he turned his thoughts to either a foster home or a group home. His plan was to finish high school and get some sort of computer programming experience for work. Then he wanted to get his own place and bring his siblings back together with him in charge.

It wasn't a bad idea, as long as he realized that his thoughts created his reality. He would have to project a positive attitude in order for him to carry out this plan. Also high on his agenda was finding a girl who would share his idea for the future. He took every opportunity to meet someone. The library was a good place to meet, and, in fact he did meet a girl there and started calling her. She was sending him little notes, and it was getting him all hyped up.

The line staff at his house had to terminate this communication, however, because Eli was becoming uncontrollable. This was another blow to Eli because he desperately wanted to see this girl. The one thing that Eli had going for him was school; he had a B+ average. Eli knew what he had to do to get to the next level in the program and he was determined to make it happen. He wanted to be moved to a more independent living residence, because that was the last step before he went to a group home out in the community.

He was being considered for a step down, and he knew it. He was working hard to follow the rules to make this a reality. In this new house, he would have more freedom, and he could even get a part-time job off campus. This would allow more opportunities for him to see his girlfriend, and that was a big motivator for him. This was an attainable goal that he could actually see happening in the near future, and it was enough to keep him moving in that direction.

If he were to move to this new independent living situation, he would be out of my jurisdiction, because it was outside of the unit I was working in. This meant that we would have to terminate our sessions. We discussed this at length and he was well aware of the outcome. He continued to plan for this change, and we started the termination process. Eli said he was ready for the move, and, by all outward appearances, it looked like a favorable prospect to everyone involved. Change felt like progress to Eli, and that was helping him feel better about himself. He had improved tremendously since that first encounter of the boy huddled in the corner howling like a dog.

He had mourned his mother's death, come to terms with his losses, and developed a connection to Lamar and me. He maintained contact with his siblings and was doing well in school. So, by all outward indicators, he had done well with the program.

He was still angry and impulsive and hated the system. He cursed God for everything that had happened to him and blamed him for his misfortunes. These things would not change overnight but, now, at least he felt he was ready to move forward. I would be angry too if I were in his shoes.

I helped him find a release for these angry emotions by acting as a sounding board for him and by validating his feelings. Overtime, I felt that these feelings would diminish. It would just have to take its own course, like the mourning process; you can't put a time frame on it. So the agency set the wheels in motion for Eli to go to this new unit, and we all planned accordingly.

Lamar and I had a going-away party for him. Even though he was only moving to the other side of the campus, it was a big step. The party also served as a container for him to have closure on the work we all had done. Furthermore, Lamar needed to see that movement was possible and that hard work paid off. He also needed to say goodbye to his friend. They would see each other from time to time, but it wouldn't be that often, and they wouldn't be sharing the studio any longer.

Both boys had tremendous loss in their life, and they each dealt with it in their own way. They were like two warriors fighting a battle that they both needed to win in order to survive. They had a mutual respect for each other and understood each other's pain. They were a witness to each other's journey, working through their despair, and they helped each other pick up the pieces of what was left after unspeakable trauma and loss.

The party was a success. Lamar was able to say goodbye in a way that tied up any lose ends. Eli was celebrated for his accomplishments and from all outward appearances he seemed to thoroughly enjoy all of the attention. He was now ready to finalize his involvement with me in a healthy way and move on.

Continuing the Fight Alone

LAMAR WAS FRAGILE AND had to endure the further loss of his friend Eli. He also had to say goodbye to his long-term psychologist, who was moving to another unit and terminating her case with him. He was profoundly affected by this, and, the day he found out, he came running to my office to tell me that she was leaving.

He said to me, "Ms. G., you are the only one I have left who I can depend on." He was shaking, and he felt as if he would fall apart. I told him that I was still there and not planning to go anywhere; my door was always open, and he could come and call on me anytime.

The staff at his house was also constantly moving around or leaving, Lamar felt like he was on a raft in the middle of the ocean, continuously being tossed around. He was forever adjusting to change. I told him that change was the only thing that was constant in life. The fact is everything is always shifting as soon as you get comfortable with one thing it changes and you have to start all over again getting used to something new. The longer you live the more you become aware of that fact.

Who ever thought that the World Trade Center would come tumbling down or that a tsunami would hit the shore of Japan causing a near nuclear disaster? But these things did happen. People die, move, and get sick sometimes unexpectedly. Earthquakes happen in more ways than one, like when you feel like you are losing your footing and can't get back on solid ground. So what do you do? Do you give up? No! You pick yourself up and move on, lending a hand to the next guy as you walk down the road.

I said to Lamar, "I am here now; that is true, and I'll help you out as long as I can. But I might not always be here. You have to always make new relationships and find people like me along the way who will help you. There will always be people out there to help because that is human nature. In turn, you will be there for the next guy; that's how it works.

You have been through a tough time because, at a very young age, the people you counted on to be there for you weren't. So you learned that, sometimes, you have to make decisions on your own and be self-sufficient. In the long run, you are the one who will be stronger for it. When the tsunami hits, you're going to be the guy who gets up and goes on because you have been in training for this since day one. It's not always about the event of change but what you do with it that counts. Learn to be proactive and not reactive; learn to see the wave coming before it hits."

I couldn't tell him that I felt as if I might not be around much longer, if another person in his life was leaving, it would be too much for him to take. But, soon, I would pick the right time and place to tell him. I needed time to prepare him for whatever loss might come his way. So for now, I told him that I would be there to help him through it.

Things on the campus were changing as well. The new special project manager working with the Rec. Department was taking on more and more art therapy interns. After I had gone to the CEO and made a proposal for the expansion of the Art Therapy Department to take on interns, he went and took my idea to someone else. Apparently, this new coordinator would supervise the interns as part of her regular duties for the Rec. Department. I couldn't do that. I needed to be compensated for my time and wanted to get a raise for supervising. I was only being paid an entry level salary.

When I came to the position I was still a student, and so I felt at that time that being a paid intern while I was still in school was a plus, sort of an on-the-job training position with benefits. But after being there for four and a half years, acquiring my license and master's degree, I felt I had earned a professional salary. The HR Department didn't see it that way; they said they never required me to go on for higher education and that if that was what I wanted to do fine, but not to ask them to compensate me for it.

I told them I never asked anyone to pay for anything. The fact was that I had to get my license in order to legally practice in my state. They felt that I just went ahead on my own. As far as they were concerned I could continue to work under a licensed psychologist, and they would be under no urgency to have me get credentialed, which was not the state's position. I made sure that I had all of my documents in order and was held to the standard that my profession required, if not my employer.

The point was that a lot of art therapists were being underpaid; I felt strongly that I needed to stand my ground and elevate the attitude toward art therapy in general if not for myself then for anyone who might come after me. The bottom line was that they didn't need me any longer; they were getting art therapy interns coming to the campus via the Recreation Department. There was no incentive to keep me on and pay me more money if they could get the same service in house.

I had the feeling that my days were numbered there, so I started looking for other options. But, in the meantime, I wanted to service the boys who were entrusted to my care. I had to be there for them and do the best job that I could do, with or without the support of the administration.

They had no cause to fire me, I was doing a great job and they knew it. Beside I didn't have the heart to leave now, not when Lamar was about to make a move. I would wait until something changed in his situation then I would consider leaving.

Lamar's behavior had improved a lot in his house. Now that he was fourteen he could get a part-time job. I remember the first time he went for a job interview; he came to show me how nice he looked wearing a suit. I must say he looked very grown up and handsome. He was so proud to be going on an interview. He was such a good kid. I was sure he would do well.

Lamar was also going to transition out of the school in the house to the big school on campus. This was a big step for him in order to eventually go to a public school off campus. If he did well in the high school, he would transition off campus to a group home or a therapeutic foster home in the community.

This was big, a very big move for a young man who had been stuck for so long. For the administration to even consider moving Lamar to the high school was a sign that he was improving. He had been schooled in house for three years because his behavior was so erratic. Ever since he came here to this agency, all the teachers had gone to him. Staying in a small group was the only way Lamar could learn.

Lamar was actually very bright and loved to read; he had read all of the Harry Potter books, and he loved biographies. I would bring him additional biographies to read, especially stories about sports figures, and basketball players like Michael Jordan and Allen Iverson.

He also went to the library every week to get books. It was his attention span that got him into trouble; he could focus on reading a book that he liked, but he couldn't just be part of a group. Now, however, he was doing better, maturing, and his grades had gone up; his behavior had improved. It was now or never for him and we were all rooting for him.

Lamar was very excited about transitioning to the big school. This would open up a whole new world to him. It seemed to be the change I was looking for, an opportunity for him to transition out of my unit on a positive note.

The thought of living with a family had filled him with hope, and his mood was more positive. At the same time, they had started to reduce his medication. It would be a real win for him if he could move to a therapeutic foster home and be free of taking any psychotropic drugs.

There were times when he would get those old pangs of guilt and remorse, but overall his outlook on life was optimistic. After all, he had been through the worst of times; I didn't think he would go back to those dark days, so from here on out everything would be on the upswing.

The one thing that kept haunting him was that he felt his mother didn't love him enough to give up her alleged drug addiction. What I told him was that was not her problem. She loved him as much as she could. She apparently didn't love herself enough to give up her drug addiction. Now that he was older, he began to understand the gravity of that statement. What seemed to upset Lamar was that he felt that he wasn't good enough, and, that he was damaged goods that no one else would want. I reminded Lamar that no one goes through this world without being tarnished in some way, because we are all human and there isn't anyone who is perfect. But what make us stronger are the trials we have to endure.

Part of my job was to highlight, for Lamar what his good qualities were. What had transpired before was not his fault. He was caught in a web of destruction that he could only react to for his own survival.

He was funny, smart, athletic, loving, compassionate, and an all-around great kid. It was a hard sell, and, most of the time, he wasn't buying it, because the bottom line for Lamar was, "Why would anyone else love me if even my own mother didn't?"

When I first met Lamar four and a half years ago, he couldn't focus or relax at all. He was so hyper-vigilant he couldn't let his guard down for a second. Now, he could contain and control himself long enough for me to teach him relaxation exercises. I felt this would help him to self-regulate in times of crises, to help him focus, breathe, and calm himself down.

We started the visualization exercise with deep breathing. I started this new process with the same exercise I had used with Alessandro called, meeting the dragon. I had no idea what would transpire, but the information retrieved would indicate how he would face his fears in the future, and if he was going to be leaving the agency, we needed to find out how he would react to stressful stimuli.

I read through my script, taking him on a journey through the woods until he saw a clearing. On the other side of the clearing was a mountain that he needed to climb to get to the cave. He climbed the mountain until he got to the cave. What happened next was truly amazing.

Lamar entered the cave cautiously, it was dimly lit but he could see that there were cave paintings and charcoal drawings on the walls. He knew instinctively that he was in an ancient place. He heard chanting coming from deep inside the cave so he followed the sound and light, which he discovered was from lit torches. He entered a large room deep inside the cave where he met a council of elders dressed in long robes. They acknowledged his presence and welcomed him into the circle. There were about twenty men, and they seemed very happy to see him, patting him on the back and telling him he was the chosen one.

First, they give him food to nourish him which gave him strength, and then they gave him a sword, a shield, and a bow and arrow. These were the things he would need to fight the dragon. After they talked to him for awhile, they sent him out to find the dragon. Evidently, the dragon was not in the cave but out in the wilderness, and Lamar had to go and find him.

He found him not too far from the cave. He was not afraid, and was able to look the dragon in the eye and stand his ground. He fought him but didn't kill him. He showed compassion for the beast but cut him up pretty badly. He wanted to show the beast that he was not intimidated by him, that he was the boss, and that he wasn't going to back down.

The dragon retreated. Lamar turned and went back into the cave where the elders were waiting for him. They congratulated him for a job well done and proceeded to put a crown on his head.

This visualization was truly astounding to me. I was very proud of Lamar to think that he could face his fear and not be paralyzed or defeated by it. It seemed to me that this visualization or lucid dream of Lamar's was part of some initiation into adulthood as described in many ancient cultures, which could account for the gathering of elders.

If you have ever read "The Hero with a Thousand Faces" by Joseph Campbell or "Man and His Symbols" by Carl G. Jung, you know that since the beginning of time, there have always been initiations. This visualization seemed to tap into the eternal archetype of the initiation of the hero. This visualization seemed to represent that Lamar was given all the tools he needed to do battle with his demons and be victorious, in order to become the champion. The elders said, "You are the chosen one."

He was fearless. He was able to stand his ground and fight. He was also compassionate and didn't kill the dragon. He didn't have to because; once he had conquered his fear it had no influence over him. He showed the dragon who was boss, this liberated Lamar from the endless cycle of rejection, defeat, and fear of death. The dragon had lost his hold on him, and he wasn't afraid any longer.

In today's world, there are not many ways in which a young man can experience a rite of passage into adulthood, as in ancient times or aboriginal societies. Yet the memory of it is still carried in our DNA. Why do you think boys seek out the gang or the fraternity, in which they have to endure strenuous initiations in order to prove themselves; it is for the sole purpose of being accepted by the group and considered a man.

When we discussed the symbolism in his journey, it was interesting to Lamar how he was supported by so many elders, encouraged by the group to do battle. He wasn't alone but rather part of a community (a community of ancestors).

The dragon was not at home but out in the wilderness, making me think that his fear was out in the world somewhere outside of himself, a fear of the unknown. Lamar subsequently confessed to me that his greatest fear was to be alone, to be left homeless. Clearly, this was a reaction to his abandonment issue. Hopefully, this will never become a reality, because the elders were there representing his support network, guiding him, always there to help him, as they said he was the chosen one.

In a practical sense, the tools he was given to fight the battle were his sword, which Lamar felt represented his intellect, (cutting through ignorance), next was his shield, he felt symbolized his fearlessness, and his need to protect himself. The bow and arrow symbolic for his love and compassion, which could pierce the heart and travel great distances (like cupid). It was important to get Lamar's interpretation of what the symbols meant because it was his unconscious that gave him the symbols. It's his personal understanding of what the symbols mean to him. I could not interpret it for him.

The visualization reminded me of the knight and the wolf story that he wrote and illustrated years earlier. I suppose it was part of a larger picture, an archetype that he carried with him. It seemed to me that Lamar carried the knight's complex of having to save damsels who were in distress, (his mom). It was his code of honor that was at stake, and he couldn't fail, otherwise he would be going back on his oath.

The next step was to help Lamar discern what the best options were for his future. If his greatest fear was to be homeless, then what could he do to safeguard against that?

In our next session, I asked Lamar to draw another landscape. In this landscape, he drew a road that ended by splitting up into several different roads all going in different directions. This seemed to represent the different possibilities he had to choose from.

Next we analyzed these choices. The best choice I felt was for Lamar to go on for higher education; he agreed. Lamar said, he wanted to study law. I felt that he was smart enough to do that, but the question remained as to how he would accomplish it.

He felt he could do it by getting a basketball scholarship. To be honest, I didn't know how good he was in basketball, and, in order for the scouts to see him he would have to go to a district school. They would never see him play here at this campus.

He was moving in the right direction to realize his dream by moving to the high school here on the campus; it was the first step. If he did well there he would be eligible for a therapeutic foster home out in the community and a district school. If he could find a high schools that had the best basketball team it would offer him the exposure of being seen by a college scout.

Lamar liked this plan because it gave him something to work toward. He knew which schools had the best teams and he had some say in where he would wind up. He now had something tangible, a plan with a direction which would put him on the right road. This plan was within his control. It gave him the confidence he needed and now he felt he was in the driver's seat.

Choices

$\mathcal{I}$T SEEMED AS IF I would never be able to expand the art therapy program the way I wanted to and I wasn't being considered for supervising interns. I had developed goals for a sound therapeutic program which offered art therapy to a wider audience but it fell on deaf ears. I couldn't see how I could continue the way I was with limited resources and no possibility of advancement.

I had to take responsibility for my role in creating my own experience, especially in not being able to convince the administration that I was the right person for the job. Art therapy didn't seem to be mainstream enough for this particular agency and I wasn't a good enough sales person to sell it to them. I didn't have a way to bring money into the agency that would support the work I was doing and the bottom line was there was no financial backing for such an ambitious project. I knew that everything happened for a reason but it was a bitter reality for me to accept at the time.

I had been thinking that I would leave the agency by the end of the school year. I knew I had to move on but I felt that I couldn't leave until Lamar was on his feet and out of harm's way.

In June, at the end of the school year, there was a good chance that Lamar would be moving to a group home. He was on the right track and focused enough to see it through. In the meantime I was sending out resumes, seeing what options were out there. I was torn up about this decision; there were so many boys on this campus that had looked to me as their anchor who I felt responsible for. I was over identifying with them, and that needed to change. I had to look at it a bit more objectively and not feel that their lives were my sole responsibility. I needed to give them the tools to survive on their own as any good therapist should do. I also needed to think about myself for once and decide what was best for me.

These boys were thwarted with loss and rejection. I didn't want to add to their list of people who walked out on them. This was the heaviness I felt of the real life dilemma I was facing. I prayed that there would be other dedicated professionals who would take up the charge after I left. I knew there were many very dedicated people on this campus, and that the boys would have to be left to their care and expertise.

The only miracle that would save my dream was if I wrote a grant that would bring money into the Art Therapy Department. Even the best grant writer in the world couldn't find that kind of money. I talked to the grant writers on the campus, and they told me the truth; there was no money out there for art. They looked and came up short. The agency knew how to find money, and if it was out there, they would have found it. Grant writing was a full-time job, and if the agency wasn't willing to go that route then I was out of luck.

So in the end after weighing all of my options I had made up my mind to leave within four months. But I didn't want anyone to know, not my supervisor or the kids. I needed to keep it to myself.

I had been asked to see a new boy who had just arrived from the street. He was in Crisis Residence because he needed to be debriefed, so to speak, from street life to residential life. I went to meet with him and offer art therapy to him as a viable resource.

While I was there, I ran into Eli. I was so surprised to find him there. I thought he was doing so well in his new "independent residence." What in the world was he doing in crisis?

I took a moment to talk with him, and, evidently, things fell apart shortly after he moved. He couldn't hold it together;

having so much freedom was too unstable for Eli. He needed the structure of the residential unit he was in before. As much as he complained about it he needed it. He was too impulsive with girls and inappropriate with them and that's what got him into trouble. He was prone to running away to meet up with them. They couldn't contain him and the truth of the matter was Eli wasn't ready.

He was very happy to see me and asked to talk to me in private. I thought that he needed to talk about what was going on in his life and didn't want the whole unit to hear him venting. I stepped into his room out of respect for him but, was not prepared for his disgraceful behavior. He made a sexual advance towards me. I was so stunned! What was he thinking?

I said, "Eli I am old enough to be your grandmother for goodness sake." How desperate for connecting with someone was he? It was then that I knew that he needed to stay in Crisis until he could regain his composure.

He wanted desperately to return to art therapy, but I knew that, in his mind the security that he felt within the confines of the art room, the container that had kept him safe in the past was being compromised. He was confused. The trust that we had built as a professional therapist and client was misconstrued.

I spoke to my supervisor about it. We had a laugh thinking that Eli had been attracted to an older woman, but it was no laughing matter; this was very serious. He desperately needed love, he had no boundaries, and, in his confusion and desperation he was reaching out to anyone he felt he could trust.

My supervisor and I both agreed he needed to be contained and talked to by another professional on campus, preferably a male therapist.

Besides the fact that I had already decided that I would be leaving in four months, I didn't want to start opening up a wound that could not be closed back up. Eli was in a desperate mindset and needed to be hospitalized and stabilized. I was beginning to wrap up cases and not take on any more new residents. These boys had so much abandonment in their lives; I needed to hand them off one by one to secure therapeutic environments. I was in the process of terminating with as many residents as I could.

About a week later I was working late one night. It was pouring rain outside as it often does in April. It was cold and damp and I wasn't particularly in a hurry to drive home in the torrential downpour. So I was taking my time catching up on my notes.

All of a sudden there was a banging on my door. Unbeknownst to me, Eli had been transferred back to his original unit. He ran out from his house, saw my light on and came running over. He was now banging on my door, pleading with me to let him in. He was screaming, "Ms. G. I can't take it anymore! I'm going to kill myself! It's no use. My life is over. I need to talk to you." Well, I have never turned anyone away in their time of need, so I opened the door and let him in.

I thought, "My God, this boy is really suicidal. He needs to be in medical." I should have picked up the phone right then and there, but I didn't. I thought I could calm him down. I was afraid he would run away again. I could see in his face the torment he was dealing with. He was upset, dripping wet and shaking.

I said, "Please come in, sit down and dry off." He said he had reached the end of his rope. I said, "All right, calm down; nothing is going to happen tonight. Tell me what's troubling you."

He couldn't sit down. He was too agitated. He just paced up and down. He came over to me and tried to grab me. I told him sit on the other side of the room, I had to call security to come and take him away. I tried to talk to him but he came at me again I went to the phone to call security.

While I was on the phone he came up and grabbed me a third time. I pushed him away and said, "Eli, you have to leave.

I can't help you when you're like this." He followed me to the door, but before I could get the door open, he turned back on me and pushed me hard against the door.

I started to get away and ran back to the phone. He then pushed me to the floor and threw himself on top of me. He was strong and hard to push away. Out of the corner of my eye I could see my umbrella leaning up against the wall. I reached out for it and managed to use it as a wedge to push him away from me. I yelled, "Stop this!" and was loud enough to scare him off. He ran out the door into the dark night, back into the driving rain.

I was shaking by this time. I went into my car and locked the doors. I was so upset thinking how desperate he had become and how he came to me knowing that I was the one person on campus who cared about him. But he was so confused. He was so desperate for love; he couldn't distinguish the love of a girlfriend from the care of a therapist.

I called my supervisor and told her that I had just been attacked by Eli. She told me to go to medical and get checked out. The next thing they had to do was find Eli. I told her that he said he wanted to kill himself.

She understood immediately how serious this was. She needed to find him before he hurt himself or someone else. I was pretty shaken. I didn't even realize the bruises that I had until the nurse got a good look at me.

My knee was swollen and I had a welt on my back from where the door knob was jammed into me. My arms had cuts and bruises on them as well, but nothing was broken.

I was instructed to go to the police and file a report. It was going to be a long night. I told them that he was dangerous and needed to be in a locked facility but I didn't want to press charges against him. He didn't need to go to jail; he needed to go to a psychiatric hospital. There were so many thoughts going through my mind I couldn't think straight. I needed to take the rest of the week off.

When I returned to campus I met with the social worker supervisor. I was informed that the art room was considered off limits. I was not to see any of the boys there alone. If I wanted to see them I would have to go to their houses. Management felt that I was too isolated and alone in my studio, that I was vulnerable to repeated attacks if I stayed there.

I couldn't believe my ears. I said in my defense that Eli was the only boy who presented a problem. He was the one that couldn't be trusted not me. But the administration didn't want to hear about it. I was speechless. I was back to working out of my car, visiting the boys in their houses just as I had done when I first arrived on campus. All of my hard work to build up my dream studio was all going down the drain. I still had two months to go before the end of school. I didn't know if I could hold on that long.

I thought if I had the interns coming in the way I had planned, then I would not have be alone in the studio that night. If only I could get the administration to listen to me. I had always known that art therapy was at the bottom of their list of priorities. I should have aligned myself with the Rec. Department when I had the chance. I could have had my plan and implemented it the way I had envisioned. But since I was told it was strictly forbidden to do any art therapy in Rec. I turned down the offer to run special projects. I didn't think I could do both. I hadn't considered taking on interns at that time, but it would have been a logical choice. I had only myself to blame. I was too myopic, a purest. I hadn't seen the whole picture. I should have known that there would be more than enough money for all kinds of projects though the Rec. Department.

I needed to grow up and stop these idealistic Pollyanna notions that the world operated on the premise of good intentions. The world operated on the bottom line. Money makes the world go around, and that is where you have to go if you want anything to take hold and flourish. I was just looking at the day-to-day needs of the kids and only took their concerns to heart, not looking out for my own interests. I just wanted to do art that is all I ever wanted to do.

I went to HR and told them that I would leave at the end of June but they had other ideas. They gave me twenty-four hours to pack up my things and leave the campus.

That gave me little time to pack up the art room with all of my books and personal belongings. Even though I had planned on leaving, I felt very let down. There was just one thing left to do. I needed to say goodbye to Lamar.

I found him out on the baseball field playing. I called over to him, told him that I needed to talk to him. He came running over. I said I've been asked to leave and that I had until the end of the day to pack up my things. They took my keys and my ID badge and I had to leave the campus. He was stunned.

I told him that I would never forget him, that I was very sorry to have to go but that I didn't have a choice. I told him to stick with the plan, not to give up, and that I believed in him, that I knew he would make it. I had done all I could for him, it was up to him now to carry on without me.

He shook his head as if he knew the drill. He was ready to put the plan into action. I couldn't help being upset. I gave him a hug and said one more time that I would never forget him; that was a promise and I never have. Then I got into my car and drove away with a lump in my throat and a heavy heart.

By the end of that month, I found out the Lamar had left the campus and moved to a therapeutic foster home somewhere in the county. I don't know what happened to Eli other than he was last seen in a psychiatric hospital.

Some kids can't overcome the emotional damage done to them; some, like Lamar are able to pull it together and make it. The difference between the two was whether or not they were able to implement a plan toward change.

Lamar was eventually able to tell his mother that he didn't need to be put into harm's way any longer and that he couldn't save her; she had to save herself. Eli was never able to fully bury his mother and he couldn't love himself enough. He was always looking for someone else to fill that void in him. It comes down to responsibility and whether or not you can be responsible for yourself.

One thing I tried to do was give the residents the tools to advance themselves without them feeling as if I was going to do it for them. They all needed to do it for themselves. Encouraging growth with sound boundaries in place; that is the only way to produce sound results, being there for them without having them become dependent on you.

It is a fine line, because they are looking for you to save them. But in reality they are the ones that have to save themselves. All you can do is to show them the way.

The forgotten boys, you see them bagging your groceries at the checkout line or scuffling their feet as they walk down the street, or hiding in doorways. These are the kids no one wants or the ones whom parents can't afford to keep. The throwaway kids that wind up homeless, living under the bridges or in boarded up old condemned buildings.

These kids eventually grow up. Some will find their way doing menial jobs. If they're smart, they will figure out a way to finish school and get a decent job. Most of them become part of the mental health system. Some find their way into the welfare system or become wards of the state. Some fill our jails or detention centers or just die on the side of the road.

These are lost boys who go mostly unnoticed because they are too painful to see. Society doesn't want to acknowledge them because then we would be forced to acknowledge that the system was broken, "Where had it gone wrong? This is the richest country in the world, how could we have poor, homeless kids living in the streets? It's not my fault that they are there, or is it?"

The fact is that the system really is broken. We live in a society that caters to the rich and turns a blind eye to the poor. The schism between rich and poor is widening in this country, and it's time we started to change the way things are. I never thought before that money could make such a difference in a kid's life. But now I think that everything is connected we are all connected. Society is a whole organic living breathing body you can't separate people into little sterilized blocks, we have to all live together and help each other.

When I look back over the four and a half years that I worked with those boys, I realized that they probably taught me more than I taught them. They were all warriors with battle scars of untold proportions, just like me. We all have scars; some you could see, and some you can't.

I will never forget them. I must have treated over one hundred kids while I was there. If ten of them make it and live to see a better day I will feel as if I did a worthwhile thing. I pray for all of them that they find some happiness in their lives, and thank God for the dedicated men and women, the many skillful and dedicated professionals, who put their lives on the line everyday to work with them. Education is a big part of the continued success for these kids. It is necessary that they be able to live in an environment where they can be kids, to play and laugh and be silly and just have fun.

Parents need to learn how to parent and be able to support their children. Kids shouldn't be having kids. Birth control is tantamount to saving children from a life of abuse and rejection.

An unwanted child is the beginning of a life of misery. Just because a girl gets pregnant does not mean she is ready or qualified to be a mother. Adults must be able to choose how many children they can physically, emotionally and financially take care of. The welfare system needs to educate women on how many children they can realistically afford to raise.

I worked with a young boy of twelve once, whose mother was a crack addict. He came to me one day crying saying, "why me why me"? What have I done to deserve such a mother? Why do I have to have a mother like this? What have I done?" It made me stop and think. "Why, what had he done?" I didn't have an answer for him.

I do feel, however, that we are all born to a particular time and place for a reason. Lives are not random, rather carefully orchestrated events that fulfill each individual destiny. The parents and families we are born into are part of a grand scheme which is part of our karmic inheritance in order for us learn and grow.

Freud indicated in his theory, on repetition compulsion states, that when a person does not integrate his or her trauma they are doomed to repeat it. The aim of this continual reenactment is to gain mastery over the very thing that causes their suffering. I believe this is not limited to just our own experience but is rather handed down from generation to generation. Understanding your ancestral heritage can help you to understand the schemas that were put into place long before you were even born.

No matter what the lesson is for you to learn while in this lifetime, you can master it, understand its influence over you, and resolve it; if you are brave enough to address your particular issues as Tyler Perry did by saying, "It stops with me.

It is not easy to say the cycle ends here and now. I want to rewrite the script and move on. Guilt is especially difficult to erase as we have seen by the example of Lamar; once you understand where the guilt comes from, you have a better chance of unraveling your fixation with it.

A wanted and loved child will be a happy, healthy, and productive adult. And an unwanted child is prone to problems because the prenatal influences develop in the brain from conception onward. A mother who is stressed passes this pathology onto the fetus. (Zeitgeist: (2011). *Moving Forward*)

Was this what happened to the mother of the twelve-year-old boy who I worked with? Where did the neglect start? How many generations had the stressor been passed down to eventually wind up causing this woman to seek out drugs as the only reprieve from oppression and poverty?

In 1944, the Nazis took all the food from Holland and sent it to the troops in Germany. The result of that diversion was particularly hard on the pregnant women and their unborn children. The babies who were in the second and third trimester of their development in what is now known as "The Dutch Hunger Winter" were babies who learned to store sugars and fats in utero because of the starvation syndrome (Zeitgeist: (2011). *Moving Forward*).

I met a woman whose mother was a child in Holland during the Dutch Hunger Winter. She was upset that she had been putting on weight and wasn't able to lose it no matter what she did. She then went on to tell me her story of how her parents had lived through the Dutch Hunger Winter. Even though her mother had survived the disaster, her body learned how to store sugars and fats in case of not having enough food.

It made perfect sense that she passed this memory on to her daughter. Fast forward fifty years, those same children are prone to diabetes and obesity as adults because they had been programmed to store nutrients by the brain's survival encoding, just as my friend had described to me. (Zeitgeist: (2011). *Moving Forward*)

The body remembers everything emotionally, physically, and psychologically. I believe this information is passed on for untold generations. As was discussed earlier, memories are passed on from slavery, Nazi Germany, wars, famines, and natural disasters (Woolger, 1988).

It's simple, really. What one mother doesn't do or can't do, takes a village to put back together. It is very difficult to change the encoding of the brain if it has been altered from stressors that occurred before the child was even born.

How many children have been born addicted to cocaine or alcohol? According to the U.S. Federal Bureau of Statistical Records 320,000 babies are born exposed to alcohol and illicit drugs while in utero each year. This seems to be a growing problem in the United States, and the need for early detection and intervention is important if we are to stem the tide of escalating birth defects. These children are usually underweight, have learning disabilities and/or physical disabilities, and are more likely to develop addictions in their adult life (Children's Bureau, U. S. Depart. of Health & Human Services).

Then there is the violent gene, which Dr. James Gilligan of Harvard Medical School has identified. There is an abnormal gene in children which causes violent behavior. But this gene is only activated if they have also been abused as children. In other words, many people may possess this gene, but the violent behavior is only activated under the right conditions (J. Gilligan, 2001).

Each person has their own threshold, but once the threshold is reached, they then go into full-blown antisocial, maladaptive behavior. In the brain, abuse actually causes genetic changes and causes the individual to stay in the brain stem, the most primitive part of the brain, in order to detect threats and help them survive.

If you are forced to remain in the limbic system or brain stem you may never develop the frontal lobe part of the brain, which is the executive functional part. This part can choose between good and bad actions (or better and best), override and suppress unacceptable social responses, and determine similarities and differences between things or events (Perry, 2006).

A child knows when he is being manipulated or coerced; he knows what is real and what is manufactured, especially when stuck in the brain stem part of the brain. More often than not, this child will react instinctively instead of intellectually, or rationally, to a situation.

There is hope however, Dr. Perry, MD, PhD, author of The Boy Who Was Raised as a Dog, states that the systems in the brain that gets repeatedly activated will change, and the systems in your brain that doesn't get activated won't change. This is good news for therapists who are trying to work with children that are stuck in their brain stems who have inherited predispositions to familial syndromes.

Dr. Perry feels that repetition is the key to changing the neural pathways in the brain. To change the thought processes in the brain that were developed by a pattern of repeated abuse, repetition is needed in modeling normal behavior, and thinking processes need to be modeled continuously until new neural pathways can be developed.

He states, "The longer the period of trauma, or the more extreme the trauma, the greater the numbers of repetitions are required to regain balance" (Perry, 2006, p. 245).

If we know that the developing brains are influenced from their immediate surroundings from inception onward, it would stand to reason that a concerted effort is needed to secure safe, stress-free homes in which to raise our children.

Insecurity about not getting your basic needs met, such as having food and shelter, are the biggest stressors a human can face. Yet, in our culture, these are the very things that are being tampered with, and that is the basis of our crumbling society. Eighteen thousand children die every day from starvation in the world, and that seems to me to be a pretty big stressor (Children's Bureau, U. S. Depart. of Health & Human Services).

Famines are not caused by lack of food but by the lack of money to purchase the food. This is a very basic need that every human has and the basis of our very survival. Can we start tackling that one need and work our way up from there? As stated by Gandhi "The deadliest form of violence is poverty." Americans have to wake up to the fact that there are millions of children, right here in the United States, who go to bed hungry every night. This has a ripple effect in the breakdown of the family unit, abuse, neglect, drug use, suicide, depression, and so on.

There were 30 million people put out of work by the 2008 financial meltdown here in the United States. This made a bad situation much worse and it's a situation that could have been avoided. There were six million foreclosures in 2010 and more in 2011 and perhaps as many as nine million in 2012. Where are all of these displaced people going to go? (Zeitgeist: (2011). *Moving Forward*)

Each person needs to take responsibility of their own finances and an increase in the minimum wage would be a great help. Support local banks and credit unions. Shop locally, buy from your local farmers, support your local businesses, and give back when you can. Pick one charity to support, like a local food bank, or give to building shelters for the homeless. Take in a foster kid who needs a home or become a big brother or big sister to a forgotten child.

There are things you can do as an individual; don't ever think you don't matter because you do. We are our brother's keeper. Say hello to your neighbor, they may need your help, but you will never find out if you don't talk to them.

If you think this has nothing to do with mental illness, neglect, depression, or drug abuse, I think you are mistaken. A society has to be looked at as a whole entity. If one is sick, we are all sick; if one falls we all fall. This is a holistic approach to the way we live now. Isolation just breeds descent, loneliness, and illness.

As far as my work with the boys I learned to see our society in a different light. These kids are not to be feared, turned away from or cast out. They need to be brought in, accepted, and loved.

As Far as I Know:

ALESSANDRO EVENTUALLY MOVED BACK home to live with his dad and grandfather. While his grandfather was still a big influence in Alessandro's life, his dad had to step up to the foreground and take his parenting role seriously, and he did. Shane was on the road to independence staying in school and working toward a career in the arts. Lamar moved to a group home and into the public school system. I can only hope and pray that he goes to college and realizes his dream. Eli needed to stabilize and find an anchor, probably in a psychiatric hospital, until he could regain his equilibrium.

Many of the boys I worked with over the years have become responsible adults. They needed a lot of support because it is not a quick fix; it never is. But when the boys felt included, accepted and loved, they began to turn it around.

What would have happened if Alessandro's parents had gotten help early on in their relationship with family counseling? Would that have made a difference?

Shane's family was in trouble because of poverty. His father was an alcoholic, and his mother couldn't cope on her own. What if she had support from family and community? Would it have made a difference?

Lamar's mother was an alleged drug addict. What had happened to her in her life that sent her down that road? Was she abused as a child? Did she feel trapped in poverty and become so disillusioned that she just gave up?

Then we come to Eli, his mother stricken with a life-threatening illness with no family around to help. Where was their support network? When you don't have money to get quality health care, horrible things can happen. His father appeared to be unstable and the stress of his wife's illness seemed to send him over the edge.

These small children were left without a safety net, no resources and no one to turn to. It is hard for just one man or one woman to support the needs of too many children. The statistics show that a single mother raising children on her own is more the norm now than it has been in previous years.

According to James Gilligan, in his book entitled, Preventing Violence, he states that (p. 77) factors that correlate with violence in the US is the rate of single-parent families: Children raised in them are more likely to be abused, and are more likely to become delinquent and criminal as they grow older. He should know because he has been studying violence for 20 years and was in charge of the pineal system in Massachusetts.

Interestingly, Gilligan compares Sweden and the US in statistics and finds that even though the rate of single mothers there is equal to that of the US the rate of violence is 1/10 that of the US. He says in Sweden there are more government programs in place to help single mothers get education, including vocational job training and they have help in finding jobs. Also there are free yes I said "free" access to high quality childcare, so mothers can work without leaving their children uncared for (Gilligan, 2001).

Our society has to help these women; we need to come together on this issue. If Sweden can do it, I think we should be able to do it here in the US.

This is America. We can expect to have a better social standing. Communities can be supportive of young women. Women themselves can be proactive and reach out to help each other, to share the burden of childrearing.

Each one of us has a responsibility to reach out to someone in need. Never settle for status quo, reach for the stars, know that you can make a difference, and things will change. What you think, you create, so think big.

References

Allan, J. (1988). *Inscapes of the child's world*. Dallas: Spring Publications

Campbell, J. (1972). *The hero with a thousand faces*. Princeton, NJ: Princeton University Press

Freud, Z. as quoted in *Psychiatric Clinics of North America*, Volume 12, Number 2, Pages 389-411, June 1989.

Children's Bureau, U.S. Department of Health & Human Services.

Gantt, L., & Tabone, C. (1998). *The Formal Elements of Art Therapy Scale: The Rating Manual*. Gargoyle Press, Morgantown, SV.

Gawain, Shakti, (1978) *Creative visualization*. New York: Bantam New Age Books.

Gilligan, J. (2001) *Preventing violence,* New York: Thames & Hudson Publishers

Herman, J. L. (1992). *Trauma and recovery.* New York: Basic Books.

Jung, C. G. (1964). *Man and his symbols,* New York: Dell Publishing,

Krippner, S.*(1990).* *Dreamtime and dreamwork.* Los Angeles, CA: Jeremy P. Tarcher, Inc.

Naparstek, B. (2004). *Invisible heroes.* New York: Bantam Books

Perry, B. (2006). *The boy who was raised as a dog,* New York: Basic Books

Sam, J. & Carson, D. (1988). *Medicine Cards.* Santa Fe, N. M: Bear & Company

Scaer R. C. (2001). *The body bears the burden.* The Haworth Press, Binghamton, NY

Williams, M.B. & Poijula, S. (2002). *The PTSD workbook.* Oakland CA: New Harbinger Publications, Inc.

Woolger, Roger J. (1988) *Other lives other selves,* London: Bantam Books

Wolpe, J. (1958). *Psychotherapy by reciprocal inhibition.* Stanford, CA: Stanford University Press.

Van Der Kolk, B. A. (1988). The trauma spectrum: The interaction for biological and social events in the genesis of the trauma response. *Journal of Traumatic Stress,* 1(3), 273-290.

Zeitgeist: (2011). *Moving Forward* zeitgeist+2011&oq=Zeitgiest& aq=2s&aqi=gs10&aql=&gs_l=youtube.1.2.0i10l10.1438.977 6.0.13836.11.9.1.1.1.0.89.6 00.9.9.0 . . . 0.0.

Ms. DePietro is an artist, art therapist, regression therapist, muralist, and writer. She has shown her artwork nationally and internationally. After working in her studio for many years as a gallery painter she felt compelled to do more to help alleviate the suffering she saw around her. Since acquiring her (LCAT) Licensed Creative Arts Therapist certification she has worked using her knowledge of the creative process to help orphaned and displaced youth. She has a studio and private practice in upstate New York, providing therapeutic counseling, and regression therapy to children and adults specializing in trauma related disturbances. She continues to paint and lives and works in the Hudson Valley inspired by the beautiful bucolic landscapes that surrounds her.

For information about workshops and lectures or how to get MP3's of the guided imagery tapes used in this book go to: www.artstosee.com

|

15
22 - 23
57
65